W9-BNJ-218

SWOLLEN

SWOLLEN

melissa lion

Published by
Wendy Lamb Books
an imprint of
Random House Children's Books
a division of Random House, Inc.
New York

Copyright © 2004 by Melissa Lion

Jacket illustration copyright © 2004 by Nonstock/Lui Lennox

All rights reserved. No part of this book may be reproduced or transmitted in any form or by any means, electronic or mechanical, including photocopying, recording, or by any information storage and retrieval system, without the written permission of the publisher, except where permitted by law.

Wendy Lamb Books is a trademark of Random House, Inc.

Visit us on the Web! www.randomhouse.com/teens
Educators and librarians, for a variety of teaching tools, visit us at
www.randomhouse.com/teachers

Library of Congress Cataloging-in-Publication Data
Lion, Melissa.
Swollen / Melissa Lion.
p. cm.
Summary: A teenaged girl copes with the death of a star track and field athlete by running.
ISBN 0-385-74642-3 (trade hardcover)— ISBN 0-385-90876-8 (library binding)
[1. Running—Fiction. 2. High schools—Fiction. 3. Schools—Fiction.
4. Death—Fiction.] I. Title.
PZ7.L6633Sw 2004
[Fic]—dc22
2003019479

The text of this book is set in 11-point Palatino.

Book design by Angela Carlino

Printed in the United States of America

August 2004

10 9 8 7 6 5 4 3 2 1

BVG

For my first writing teacher, Susan Vreeland

and

For F.Y.
I think I'm finally over you.

acknowledgments

There would be no book if it weren't for Shaye Areheart, who first told me to try writing a novel. Thank you. Many thanks to my agent, Loretta Barrett, and to Allison Heiny for friendship and Nick Mullendore for keeping me sane through the process.

Thank you to my parents, Linda Helbock and Richard Harmatiuk, for throwing all kinds of support at this writing thing. And thank you to my stepdad, Steve Helbock, for believing with more passion and determination than I could muster at times.

Thank you to my friends: Theresa Moorehouse for being my first reader and the finest writer I know. Andy Hunsaker for reliving all those strange moments. The Olsons for never letting me take it too seriously. And Robert Lion, for everything.

Thank you to Alison Root for kindness and attention. And Wendy Lamb, whose careful reading, endless patience and gentle touch formed my words into a real book, thank you.

And I ran.

I ran every day. I liked hearing my blood rush behind my ears as I reached the top of the hill close to my school and I liked the blackness that clouded my eyes as I turned into the school's driveway. I ran because Coach Rose ran every day. Coach was a dark-haired woman with blue, blue eyes who loved running more than anything. She said, "Girls, you must be disciplined. Get out there on days you're too tired and days when the sun is bright and the breeze is cool and there are many beautiful things you could be doing." She made us run on hot days and days the smog level was dangerously high.

I wasn't the best, so I wasn't in the front of the pack. Those were the strong girls with long, lean muscles. They were serious about their running. They had no boyfriends and were on the periphery of popularity. They won plastic medals coated in gold or silver spray paint and they displayed them with their tennis trophies and horseback riding trophies in elaborate wooden cabinets in their bedrooms or the hallways of their sprawling single-level homes.

I wasn't one of the worst—those were the most popular girls in school. They wagged their arms across their chests and their feet made awkward circles in the air behind them as they moved forward. They were thin, very thin, and very blond. They were like small ghosts, but they often laughed loudly and hollered to get each other's attention in the halls. They wandered around the locker room in their purple and red bras and panties and talked about their periods and the nights at the glider port parked and drinking cans of beer in their boyfriends' cars. Sometimes they fainted because of the heat or because they starved themselves and ran too far, but they picked each other up and smacked each other's pale faces before Coach noticed. The rest of us kept our mouths closed. We liked the fainting days because the skinny girls were quiet in the locker room, considering the terrible things they did to their bodies.

I was a middle girl. In everything I did. I was the middle runner with a few girls behind and a few in front of me, whom I sometimes passed. I ran every day with hope that one day I would win.

And I ran because the cross-country team was the best team in the school. The boys at our school surfed and skateboarded. Nobody cared about football or basketball. Cross-country was the sport everyone watched, though there was little to see until the winners rounded the track into the stadium, their fists pumping, heads bobbing as the crowd cheered. I was JV, but I hoped one day to be varsity and to know that feeling of people rooting just for me.

chapter one

The new boy showed up on the day Owen Killgore died.

Earlier in the morning, when I walked through the quad and saw the popular girls crying and the jocks swiping at their eyes with their sweatshirt sleeves, I knew something was very wrong. I found my best friend, Chloe, sitting against a wall with the pad of her thumb pressed to her wrist, staunching a small bit of blood from a cut she'd made, thinking no one would notice.

She stood and I put my hand on her wrist over the cut as she tried to hug me.

"You promised," I said, holding tight to her wrist. "No more cutting."

"I saw his body," she said into my hair. "Owen died." I loosened my grip.

"What?" I said, and looked at her closely for a smile on her round face. Chloe's skin was pale and smooth like the inside of a shell and her eyes drooped at the corners and made her look sad.

"It's true," said Chloe.

"It can't be," I said. Not Owen Killgore. The most popular boy couldn't die. He was destined for greatness, they'd said when he was chosen homecoming king. When he won races, the boys' coach stood in front of the teams and talked about Owen's dedication and drive. Owen would bite the inside of his cheek and stare beyond the coach at a vague point on the horizon.

"He won at the last meet," I said.

It had been at our school. The girls' team had finished and we'd stretched and cooled off before the rumble started in the crowd. I sat up in the grass as the people in the stands began to cheer. A single air horn went off as Owen circled into the track. His hands were loose and he smiled as he ran past the home-side seats. He knew the cheers were for him, only him.

"It was horrible. The ambulance woke me," Chloe said now. She lived across the street from Owen. She put her arms around me and squeezed. "I just saw him in the quad yesterday playing football during lunch."

"I don't believe it," I said.

"No," she said. "He was a good person."

When they were kids, she and Owen trick-or-treated together, and splashed together in swim lessons. In her locker, Chloe kept a photo of them as kids making soap beards and mustaches in the bathtub.

"I'm so, so sorry," I said.

She pressed her lips together and nodded. "I'm sad for you guys. For cross-country."

"He was a great runner." He was lean and his stride was long, his hands and shoulders loose like he could run for days. But this beauty and this confidence were only visible from far away. Up close he was just a boy. I had found this out one afternoon a few weeks before.

The bell rang and Chloe hugged me again. "Don't be late."

I walked to first period. The spindly ceramics teacher sat on her desk and dangled one shoe off her toes.

"As you know, Owen Killgore died in his sleep this morning. He was peaceful." She wiggled her foot back into her shoe. She dusted chalk from her hands onto her thighs. "Please read, or work, or go out and talk to the counselors and be with your friends. I'm so sorry," she said, and pressed a tape into a portable stereo. Classical music played as some people got up, and I rested my head on my desk. I dug my thumbnail into a groove in the Formica and for a secret moment I felt relief that Owen was gone, because on that afternoon a few weeks ago he seemed to know me too well.

It was after a meet and I was walking up the hill to my house, which was on the opposite side of the canyon from the nicer part of town. I'd heard stories about the trails in the canyon, about a runner found raped and left for dead. About the coyotes and the homeless people who lived there.

I walked slowly as the sun heated the shirt on my back and I felt my neck burning. Owen came up from the canyon, still in his shorts and jersey. He jumped when he saw me.

"JV Girls' Cross-country, right?" he said.

"Varsity Boys' Cross-country, right?" I walked quickly,

but he walked next to me. His sweat made him look clean, like he'd stepped out of the shower.

"You don't win many races, do you?" he asked. I could smell him, wet and brown like mud and dead leaves. I stopped and the cars groaned past us up the hill.

"I don't win any, but I don't come in last either."

He stopped and touched my arm. His fingertips were cool despite the heat.

"I lost today," he said. "Not last place, but close."

"Congratulations," I said. I stepped around him and kept going. He walked beside me so close his arm brushed mine and I was suddenly hotter; his body radiated heat.

"I need to go home." I walked faster, thinking of a time in elementary school when two boys wouldn't let me pass in a corridor.

"Have you ever run the trails in the canyon?"

"I haven't," I said.

"Wanna run now? I can show you the best trail."

"Go shower up, maybe we can run another time," I said, thinking that would be enough for him. I would make plans with him, and then accidentally forget. Not just because of Owen's girlfriend, Linda, though I was sure if she knew she would kill me. But because I wasn't popular and if anything happened between me and Owen, I'd be called a slut as soon as he told all his friends.

He stopped walking and I looked at him up close for the first time. From far away he looked handsome, with dark hair and tanned skin, but now I noticed his eyes were just a bit too light for his skin—a kind of cloudy jade—and his cheekbones were too sharp. Still, he fit the idea of handsome and the girls at our school could forgive him for this.

He waited and watched me. He assumed I was fast because of some of Chloe's friends, girls who listened to music that sounded like teeth grinding and dyed their hair a deep black and wore tall boots.

Chloe's friends invited us along sometimes when they went to talk to college boys on the beach, usually because they needed an excuse for their mothers, or someone to drive them home after they had gotten drunk on Midori in their cars.

And maybe Owen had heard that on those nights I'd been with some boy who'd graduated from our school a few years before.

I stepped back from him. Owen expected me to be who he thought I was. I liked boys who were surprised by my interest. Grateful for my attention. He was a boy who got attention all the time.

"Why don't you drive me home?" I said.

"I knew it," he said, and ran back to campus to get his car. I took off, crossing the street into the apartments and condominiums. My jeans were tight on my knees and heavy from my sweat. I ran fast, through parking lots and between houses, until I reached my development. I slowed, my breath coming fast and the deafness only broken by my heartbeat in my ears. I lost myself in the tangle of streets, where the condos could only be told apart by the large blue numbers on each bundle of buildings.

After that, in school and during practice, he acted like he had before, like I was invisible.

The new boy appeared in my second-period class that day. He stood next to the teacher's desk as we filed in and took our seats, and at first I thought he was a new assistant.

I was in this class because a test I had taken in the second grade said I was gifted. I'd gotten mostly Cs in math classes since junior high, but somehow I kept getting placed in classes with the smart kids.

There were times when I would copy the board, then do my homework and be very exact, following the teacher's instructions. I'd check the answers in the back of the book and I would be right, perfect, and the ease of it all took my breath away.

This new boy walked through the aisle and sat at an empty desk next to me. He was tall, perhaps six feet, and broad, muscular without the tense definition that boys in weight training got. His strength looked natural, like he'd never had to lift a weight. And his skin was brown, warm and soft like baked bread. When our teacher introduced the boy she called him Far-ock, like "far off."

"Long *u*," he said. "Farouk." His lips pursed around the last syllable, ending it with a small breath. From him the word sounded soft and round, and I knew he was used to his name being mispronounced. He'd stopped hearing how ugly his name could be from a stranger's mouth.

"How're you doing?" he asked me. His accent was from the East Coast.

He settled his books and papers and he smiled at me again.

"I'm well, thank you," I said in a whisper.

He wore slacks and a button-down shirt with pale pink boat shoes. His nails were short and clean, and his face was well shaven, no nicks or blemishes. When he wasn't smiling at me he looked like a boy, like the little kid he was before he grew up.

The teacher said, "I know a lot of teachers are letting people out today and you may go if you please, but I'm going to conduct class. I think it is best to keep things as normal as possible despite the tragedy."

I tried to follow the equations. Farouk rarely took a note, though most of the time he watched the board like he was ready to catch the teacher in an error. And when he wasn't looking at the board he turned to me, watching me watch the board and take notes that I knew were wrong. I erased and tried to copy again but the numbers would not come out of my pencil in the right order.

Farouk opened his book and scooted his chair close to mine.

"I can help you." He drew one finger down my paper.

"I'm fine," I said, trying to erase the smudges his thumb left in the jumbled numbers.

I pretended to study and nodded like I understood.

When the bell rang, he followed me into the hall.

"Farouk," he said, and held his hand out to me.

"Samantha Pallas." I took his hand. It was the first time in a long time I had said my whole name. I squeezed his hand and looked into his eyes like my dad had taught me.

He squeezed back and let me go. "See you later," he said.

Next period our teacher led us to the gym where the bleachers had been pulled out for an assembly and the bright white lights glowed from the ceiling.

I looked for Chloe, but it wasn't until I sat in the middle

of a row halfway up that I saw her waving from a bleacher across the floor.

Farouk dropped onto the bench next to me. "Not much learning happens here," he said, sitting close.

"A boy died. He was a runner, like me," I said.

We were quiet as the principal stood in front of the microphone beneath a basketball hoop.

"Our school has suffered a tragic loss. We are all confused and saddened and so we thought it would be best to tell you all everything we know. Mr. and Mrs. Killgore would like to speak to the school." Mr. Killgore stood. Owen's mother sat still, letting tears drip into the folds of her black dress. She looked like Owen, with pale eyes and tanned skin.

"Thank you for your support today," Mr. Killgore began. "Walking the halls, I felt the camaraderie Owen often talked about. He had many friends here. It had been his dream since junior high to run with the varsity cross-country team. He considered them family." As he shifted his feet and looked around at the school, I sat up straighter. Farouk leaned his elbows into his knees.

"Owen died of heart failure. My father had heart problems and I passed them down to my son. Owen died in his sleep because his heart was swollen." A girl behind me gasped and people around me murmured to each other.

Farouk looked at me over his shoulder, raising his eyebrows.

"It's rare, but it happens," said Owen's father. "The doctor was keeping an eye on Owen. He said that the sports would help strengthen Owen's heart. But he told us there was a small risk. Each year a very small number of kids die from the same heart problems Owen had. We just couldn't have known." He shook his head and pressed his fingers to his mouth. He turned from the microphone and sat next to Owen's mother, taking her hand.

The principal stood and told us there would be grief counselors available for us.

"We are so sorry," he said, and the teachers stood and motioned for us to file out through the bleachers.

Farouk touched my arm as I stood. "We're not cattle. Wait for everyone to clear out." I sat back down.

"It wouldn't have happened that way," he said, close to my ear.

"If you're not a runner, you can't understand how fast and hard your heart gets going." I remembered a time I was running a huge hill and I felt as if my heart was pounding too hard, too deep, and it would crack my chest right open.

"That kid didn't die of heart disease." As his lip brushed my ear, in the middle of all the kids crying, I felt hope, like I would have at any secret a boy told me—I really was his first, or I was the prettiest girl he'd kissed.

"They do," I said. "Anyone can die of heart problems. There was a girl I went to elementary school with who had a lot of operations."

"Did she die?" he said.

A bell rang and I checked the clock. It was lunch, already.

I stood. "See you tomorrow."

He leaned back against the bench behind him and waved to me as I took the steps two at a time.

• • •

I found Chloe talking to Katherine, one of the girls who took us to the beaches. Like most kids at my high school, they had known each other since kindergarten. I'd arrived in the ninth grade, when I stopped living with my mom and moved into my father's condominium with him and his girlfriend, Ruth.

Chloe and I became friends on the first day of school, first period. It was drama class and the teacher asked us to pair up. Chloe wore jeans with fraying cuffs and platform sandals. I wore new jeans and my running shoes. I wanted badly to tear the bottoms of my jeans like she had.

Chloe pulled her desk next to mine. "Watch," she whispered. "As soon as she starts us on the exercise she'll go into the back room. Her booze is back there."

"You will interview your partner and write a brief speech introducing him or her," said the teacher, and then left the class. Chloe nudged me and took out a pen and paper. "Okay, Miss Pallas, give me your life story." She looked at me over imaginary glasses she had pulled down her nose.

"Hmm. Well, I live with my dad. I'm in the ninth grade. I run," I said.

"That's no life story. Tell me about getting tattoos with your truck driver sister. Tell me about performing in the circus with your fire-eating dog."

"No dogs, and I'm an only child."

"A lonely child? That's sad," she said.

"I'm an only, not a lonely. But there was the time that I climbed the Empire State Building. A giant condor had kidnapped a small boy, holding him captive in a huge nest on top, and was dangling him above the city streets. I used suction cups to climb the building. Never seen anything like it,"

I said. Chloe wrote *Empire State Building, suction cups* and *daring rescue.*

"That's what I'm looking for," she said. "As for me, I am the real owner of the British crown jewels. I stole them on my tenth birthday."

"I speak seventeen languages. *Hola, yo soy Samantha.*"

"I'm the international chess champion."

I nodded and uncapped my pen. "We've both led the most interesting and fabulous lives in this whole school," I said.

"That was obvious before class even started." Chloe and I laughed and the teacher came out with her hand covering her mouth and a smile on her face.

When the bell rang, Chloe said, "Meet me outside the library for lunch." I smiled at her with relief.

In our first year of high school, she wanted to be close to Katherine and her friends. The popular boys called them sluts, though Katherine often said, "High school boys are just that—boys. Kids. I'm not a baby-sitter."

At the beach, those girls would choose college boys—the loudest, the blondest, the boy who put his arm around a girl and grabbed her hip the fastest or hardest. And some nights there were a few boys who stood on the outside of the circle with us. Chloe would talk to them about school, or their old girlfriends, and I would find the quietest boy. The one who seemed to have nothing to say, or to laugh at, and I would talk to him about whatever he seemed to be interested in. And then I would tell him to meet me the next night.

Sometimes I would find a way back to the beach and we would walk along the water, past the bonfires that made my clothes smell warm, and later we would kiss. Some boys, the quiet boys who couldn't look me in the eye, I'd let go all the way. They always seemed so grateful to me.

Now, I laced my fingers through Chloe's and pulled her away from Katherine. Chloe's eyes were red; large pink blotches covered her neck and cheeks. She looked feverish. She hugged me, soft and warm. I felt taken care of.

"His brother was screaming on the lawn," she said, and I pictured Henry, Owen's little brother. He was younger than I was. His feet and hands looked large, as big as Owen's, but his body was thin and small, so he looked as if he was about to tip over. He carried a large backpack heavy with books, and his brown hair stood on end as if he'd just woken up. Behind his right ear he wore a hearing aid, and this made my heart break each time he scuttled by me in the hall. Now I imagined Henry, his large fists making balls next to his sides, his mouth open, screaming.

We sat on a bench in the quad where we ate, usually while the senior girls took their shirts off and sunbathed in bikini tops. But now the quad was quiet. Teachers hugged students and a group of women in business suits sat at desks near the soda machine. Students faced them and the women nodded and held their hands. The grief counselors. They looked like the mothers who helped with the newspaper drives and bake sales, now without their smocks. Always dressed appropriately for the event.

"How are you doing?" I asked.

She lifted the thick ponytail that fell down my back. Sometimes I'd threaten to cut it all off and she'd say, "I love this hair. You can't ever cut it. How will your handsome prince ever climb up and save you?"

"What was that crap about his heart? I've never heard of any sports star dying that way." Chloe shook her head. "He had a doctor. And don't they check that kind of thing in your sports physicals?"

"A nurse weighs us and takes our blood pressure."

"It's weird. If he had a bad heart, why would his parents have taken the risk and let him run?"

"A lot of people have been saying it sounds strange," I said, thinking of Farouk.

"Maybe it wasn't disease," she said. "He was winning a lot. Maybe he had help."

"Drugs?" I shook my head. "No, he really was good. He worked hard. He ran extra laps."

"He ran the cliffs near Black's Beach," said Chloe.

"He was just plain fast." He was the runner I hoped to become.

Steroids had not reached our school, though I heard rumors about stars on rival teams who were taking them. Those boys were the fastest, but their bodies looked lumpy, their muscles misshapen. Their faces were aged, leathery with patches of fine hair. These boys with their open secret looked awkward and uncomfortable until the start of a race, when they crouched down like cats and ran with the speed and confidence of grown men.

"I guess we'll never know," she said, and stood. "I'm going home; I just waited to make sure you were okay." I watched her back as she walked away. She was not as upset as she should have been. If she had been, she wouldn't have come to school at all.

• • •

As Coach Rose led us in stretching, the skinny girls cried about Owen and the best girls maintained their usual determination.

"Running will help with the grief," Coach said. "Breathe it out, sweat it out, stomp it out."

That day I ran strong and fast. I passed the middle of the pack at the halfway point. I watched the leaders' backs, their strong legs, the bottoms of their feet reaching up and back, creating long strides. That afternoon, I thought I could catch them, and I ran until my side ached. My breathing was jagged and heavy.

As we rounded the corner of the field I saw Linda, Owen's girlfriend, sitting in the bleachers. She stared at the track and pulled her fingers through her long, black hair. She dressed like a *chola,* a Mexican gangbanger, baggy white T-shirt over a black bra and tight black pants. Her eyebrows were painted into a look of sarcastic surprise and her eyes were heavy with black liquid eyeliner pointing toward her scalp.

I looked up too long and stumbled as Linda watched me.

Linda and Owen had been together forever. She was tough and fought with other girls who looked like *cholas.* Owen would grab her around the waist and carry her through the crowd before the teachers found them.

My side was pinched with a cramp, but I ran on because I felt those middle girls behind me. I only finished two steps before the pack and I shook my head as I cooled off. Linda watched as I stretched.

When the coach read our times she put her arm around my shoulder.

"Sam broke her best time. She came in three seconds faster. Such a good run!"

Alice, the fastest girl, nodded and smiled, knowing how it felt to be better than just days before. The middle girls looked at me for some clue to what I had done; then they rolled their eyes and turned their shoulders and talked to each other about how they were so close and I had jumped the start. I used to say the same thing.

"I stumbled," I said.

"Next time you won't," Coach said.

As I walked home that afternoon, I thought of the story I could tell my mom about my day: The king of the school had died. A boy who wanted to talk to me had arrived. And I had broken my best time. If I could sit down and talk to her, she'd press her thumb onto my forehead, smoothing the lines between my eyebrows, and she would say the same thing Coach Rose had said—"Don't worry. Next time you won't lose your stride. Next time you'll win." But we couldn't have that talk. My mom lived in Oakland.

"I need a change in the weather," she'd said when she told me she was moving. I was just finishing eighth grade. "I need to try a different me."

"What does *that* mean?" I said. "It's not like a pair of jeans. There aren't new yous hanging up in different parts of the world."

"Maybe there are, and we need to find them. You can come too, come live in the Bay Area with me. We'll get an apartment. You can go to the arts high school." She held her hands in her lap and picked at the skin on her thumb.

"There's nothing wrong with here. I don't mind the weather. And I'm not creative. I'm an athlete."

"So you'll go to a sports school. We'll live together again. Two girls discovering a new town."

We had lived together for a few years after my parents had broken up for good when I was ten. She was gone a lot. She went to classes at night, aerobics or poetry. The house was empty and so I spent weekends with my dad. We went to movies and hung around the house. He'd ask me how I was and if I said I was good, he'd ask me about it, but if I just said I was fine, or okay, he wouldn't press it. Unlike my mom, who would ask and ask and ask until I told her every detail about a jerky kid at school or a crappy grade on a test. It was easy to be with my dad; to just be quiet and let the scenery pass. So in the ninth grade I moved in with him after he promised me no more nights of microwaved dinners. Ruth was already living there, and I didn't realize until I moved in that it was Ruth who would make sure I had a hot dinner, not my dad.

"Dad needs me," I had said that day.

She smacked her hands on the table and sighed. "He makes you think he needs you. He's always done that so you've always wanted to protect him. He doesn't need it. He's a grown-up. He should protect you. You have a right to that. You can't be so attached." She watched me with her eyebrows creased and I wanted to press my thumb to her forehead and soften her lines. Still, I was mad.

"You can't just leave," I said. "Don't you need to plan? Find a job?"

"I have money saved. I'll find a job. When you want to move up, I'll have an extra room." And in a month she quit her job in an office, sold her things and packed up her car. She sold fancy lamps at a lamp store in Berkeley. She called every so often and told me about things like the fog coming over the Golden Gate Bridge. "I'm so happy," she said. I imagined a lot of women like my mom in Oakland. Women who wore faded Levi's, and tied their thick hair in knots.

"Finally, I have a garden. It's a community garden, but I have a little plot where I plant veggies," she'd said. I hadn't realized what she'd been missing in San Diego. I didn't know we were holding her back from planting tomatoes in an abandoned parking lot.

I decided to take her advice and not be too attached. I waited for her to call me, which wasn't often because trying new lives took a lot of time. And so now when I had something to tell her, I would tell her in my head the briefest way I could before her next phone call. Walking home after Owen had died, I had many things to say. I tried to make it simple. The most popular boy was dead. "Terrible," she'd say. "But those guys can be trouble." The new boy, Farouk, cared to hear my name. "He should want to hear more than that," she'd say. I ran faster than I ever had, but then I tripped. "You'll run even faster next time, because you'll be more careful, and more confident. And soon you'll win." She knew because when she was young, she'd been a track star. I'd found her varsity letter in an old box she was throwing out before she moved. I'd put it in my pocket and she never knew. I kept it hidden deep in a drawer.

chapter two

The next day in math class, we were supposed to exchange and check homework with the person next to us. Farouk held his paper out to me. His numbers were thin and tall, no erasures. I looked at my own paper, full of pink smears, as I handed my work to him. If he asked I would tell him the truth, that I did not belong in this class most of the time, but sometimes I did, sometimes I got lucky and understood. His paper had no mistakes, but I got half wrong.

"Tough time?" he said. When we were supposed to hand the papers back, he kept mine a second longer.

"We just started this chapter," I said with my hand out for my paper.

"We did this last year at my old school." He handed me my paper. He'd torn off a corner.

"I'll tutor you," he whispered, and handed me the corner of my paper with his phone number on it.

"I don't think so," I whispered back, trying not to smile.

He grabbed my fist and I jumped.

"I need friends," he said. He squeezed my fist. His hand was hot, sweating. And I smiled at him. He might have looked like a man, strong and confident, but with his hand making my fingertips tingle, I knew he was no different than those quiet boys on the beach.

The teacher began a new lesson about gambling, starting with slot machines. She drew an equation on the board and as she solved it she showed us how much money is lost before someone wins.

Farouk watched the board and took notes, but when I looked over his shoulder I saw they were problems with far more steps than those the teacher was doing.

The girl behind me whispered to a boy. "Linda's pregnant."

"Slut," the boy hissed. Slut. I loved that word—the way the tongue curled and the teeth showed. *Slut.* But Linda was not really a slut like Chloe's friends, or like popular girls who slept around more than Chloe's friends, but got away with it because they were the ones giving others that label. Linda had a boyfriend and she slept with him. This wasn't what sluts did. She was called that now because she wasn't cool or thin or blond.

"That's why he did it," the girl said.

"She's just a slut," said the boy again. I looked at Farouk

to see if he had heard, but he was solving his own equations.

"Even when you win, you lose," said the teacher.

Chloe waited for me outside my class and we went to lunch. She wore a coral sweater and a flowered skirt, and she looked happy, wiped clean like yesterday had never happened. We sat with our backs against the cool plaster wall of the school, and her knee rubbed mine. There was a bite to the air despite the sun and when the wind blew, if I closed my eyes, I could smell the ocean, though it was nearly ten miles away.

"Did you hear about Linda?" she said, smiling, and offered me a carrot.

"I can't believe he let her get pregnant," I said. "I can't believe this dream boy, the boy wonder, would let any girl force him into mediocrity."

"They were in love," said Chloe.

"I'm sure he loved her like he loved all those girls he hung out with in the quad," I said.

"I saw them kissing once in an empty classroom. Not making out, just kissing. He held her face and kissed her on the mouth, her eyes, and the top of her head. Very sweet." She smiled at me.

"Chloe, you're such a romantic. How will we ever keep your heart in one piece?"

Her sad eyes drooped and I wanted to touch her face, pull up those eyes so they looked happy like the rest of her.

"If you had seen them you would know. You'd believe. Carrot?" she said. I had nothing to offer her, but at that moment I would have given her anything because she was nice to me, and to the world. She truly believed in the good in people.

"I'd believe it if he weren't a boy," I said. "If he weren't the homecoming king."

"He held her hand." Chloe held her own hands together.

"Last time I checked, holding hands doesn't make a baby," I said.

"I used to see him climbing out of his window in the middle of the night to see her. He backed his car out of the driveway with the lights off."

"Oh, Chloe, spare me. He was a jock. He was the most popular guy here. He could have been going to see anyone. He probably *was* going to see anyone." If I had waited for him to get his car that afternoon it would have been me. How many other girls had he approached like that?

But I wanted to believe that there was a boy in this world who would sneak out of the house because of love and love me despite my past, a boy for whom I could give up kissing strangers at the beach. And maybe, for Chloe, Owen had been that boy.

"Did you see the new guy?" I asked. She crumpled her bag.

"I did," she said. "He's in my English class. Very handsome." When I thought of his face he looked strong, not handsome, almost fierce. His features were broad with black eyebrows, black eyes shaped like a cat's.

"He's from New York," she said, "and he read aloud from *The Grapes of Wrath.*"

"He offered to tutor me in math class," I said, and rolled my eyes.

"I saw him sitting next to you at the assembly. Maybe you should ask him to tutor you in sex ed," she said, and poked me in the side. "He's really cute."

I picked at my shoelace and tried not to smile, and when I couldn't help myself I laughed, hoping Chloe would think it was at her joke, but I knew she knew better.

She put her finger to her lips and shushed me. "We're still supposed to be upset."

I watched the quad, where the grief counselors sat, turning pink in the sun, at empty tables.

At the center table of the quad, popular girls pretended to eat, and among them sat Linda. She smiled and laughed and nodded when people talked to her. She was the only dark-haired girl, and she seemed to take up twice as much room as the others. She put her feet up on the bench opposite her and spread her lunch in front of her. Though she had moments when she looked down at the table or at her hands and wiped her eyes, she seemed happy.

The warning bell rang and Chloe gathered her things.

"Let's go out tomorrow. There's a party at a co-op at State. We'll dance on the tabletops," she said, and squeezed me, as if we weren't just returning to class but wouldn't ever see each other again. I hugged her back because I knew we would.

After school, instead of practice, the cross-country team listened to a doctor.

"If all of a sudden you become exhausted after running,

see a doctor. If your family has a history of heart conditions, please see a doctor," he said. I wanted to laugh at this little man in the girls' locker room. I could picture him in high school walking slowly past the door, hoping for a glance inside.

"Go home this evening and ask your parents for their own history and their parents' history. Although the chances for heart failure at your age are slim, it is hereditary, from the family, so information is your friend," he said.

The sweet hair spray and laundry soap smells from the girls battled the sour sweat smell of the locker room. The moisture in the air made me short of breath. I felt tricked—I had come to run, not to become afraid for my future because of my past.

He and the nurse asked us to line up, and they began measuring our blood pressure and heart rates. The doctor put the black cuff on my arm and pressed his soft fingers into my wrists. He pumped my arm until my fingers tingled and then released the pressure of the cuff. He put his cold stethoscope on my chest. He breathed deeply and I breathed deeply. He listened again at my back and I wanted to sleep, to close my eyes and let this man listen to my whole body, the blood pumping through my legs, my lungs expelling air.

"Your signs are good, but we're asking everyone to come in for X rays," he said. He gave me a card to make an appointment and went on to the next girl.

My dad and Ruth were sitting at the dining table when I walked in. My father's eyes looked red, as if he'd been crying, but he couldn't have been. The last time he cried was when my mother left.

Ruth bit at her lip.

"Sam, have a seat," she said, and patted the chair next to her. They both wore their work clothes. My father was in a suit, his bright white shirt pressed and tucked into his navy blue pants. The deep burgundy tie hung like an award around his neck.

Ruth wore a cream linen shirt with wood buttons and a long skirt to her ankles. She wore painted bracelets on her wrists and she let her red hair dry in natural waves. She was ten years younger than my dad and they worked together, so my dad insisted they keep the relationship a secret. She was unlike any other woman my dad had brought home. He liked women who wore black pumps and short skirts. But Ruth didn't need that. Her body was warm and soft when she hugged me. She had bright blue eyes and her skin glowed. When I'd asked her how she kept her skin so perfect, she'd said, "Oil of Olay since I was your age." So I asked my dad to buy it for me when he went to the store.

"Ruth heard about the boy on the cross-country team. Was he your friend?" he said.

"No, he was just a boy on the team. He was a popular boy. I'd talked to him once or twice."

"You have to tell us these things," he said. "You need to talk about it."

"We talked about it at school. I didn't know him." Our house was cool and the cold moved from my fingertips and through the rest of my body.

"Did he use drugs?" said Ruth.

"He was an athlete, a runner, not a stoner," I said. "It's really sad, but it wasn't a big enough deal to call this family meeting."

"Sam, kids that age don't die from heart trouble," said Dad.

"The doctor said Owen's heart was swollen."

"I remember hearing about a girl who played soccer dying suddenly," said Ruth. "I thought the news said it was heart disease."

"I don't remember that," said Dad.

"I do," I said sharply, and stood. I wanted to stay and be with my father, take advantage of his being home when I was home like a real parent should be. But I'd stood up and so I had to walk away because there was no way to take it back, to be un-angry. I knew he wouldn't let it drop. He would ask me again about Owen, and about why I hadn't told, and he would look at me, his forehead creased, and wonder if he was losing me. If I'd begun to keep secrets. He didn't know that I'd always had secrets.

"I don't remember and it doesn't make sense," he said as I walked up the stairs to my room.

I sat in front of my books. I opened a page and read, but couldn't follow. Instead I thought about Owen. Over the past few weeks things on the outside had seemed to be slipping from him. He hadn't won meets, and his girlfriend was pregnant. He was not himself. Owen was a winner, in perfect control of his future. When did he realize he wasn't who he thought he was? When did he know that he was not living the life he thought he was living? Did he know after his heart stopped and in the seconds his body spent turning off? Or had he realized it days before and looked into his medicine cabinet, or grabbed one of those lumpy drugged boys and asked him for enough of anything so he could be a different person, or no person at all?

I hoped his heart had simply stopped like they had said.

The next morning I walked to school listening to my own body, waiting for an unfamiliar pounding in my chest.

We had a meet in the afternoon at a high school less than a mile from the beach, built in the Mexican adobe style. The walls were cream and it sat among mansions and green lawns. The kids were very rich and they looked just slightly older, more sophisticated than we did.

The bus ride there was quiet. The boys' team looked out the windows or into their laps.

Normally their coach would stand at the front of the bus and tell us, "Make the school proud, run like you mean it." But today he sat in the front seat just behind the driver. He leaned forward, watching the cars pass us on the freeway. As we pulled into the lot, he stood, grasping the seats on either side of him, his body swaying. "Owen would want us to win this one," he said. "Win it for him. Give it everything you've got." The boys looked at him and back to their windows.

The opposing teams were already stretching as we walked onto the field. All of the girls were tan, their muscles defined. I couldn't tell who the winners were, who the slow girls were, and who'd run next to me. They all laughed together and sang the school's fight song while they huddled.

At this school we gathered in a circle, our heads together, staring at the thick green grass on their field. Even the popular girls huddled with us and while the captain talked we squeezed each other's hands.

"We are strong girls. We are winners," said the captain. "We'll all go out there and run our best, our hardest. That's how we'll win." I wanted to believe that. Maybe Owen was somewhere above us in the clear blue sky, urging me, a middle girl, to win.

At the starting line, my muscles were warm from stretching. I felt tall and proud that my legs could take me so far, so fast. When the gun sounded I ran, girls around me pumping their fists.

I began to sweat and my face turned bright red. I passed the slow girls from the other school, who were much faster than my slowest teammates. My cheeks burned as my feet hit the cement and sent tiny shocks through my calves. I focused on the backs of the girls ahead of me and on the Day-Glo ribbons flickering on trees, tied there to keep us on track.

The fast girls were yards ahead. When I reached the ocean, I watched the surfers sitting on their boards and my heart pounded.

As I ran the last stretch by the water, I took a short breath of sea air, disrupting my pattern. I was terrified and thrilled by the water, by those surfers who never seemed worried. My side pinched and I panted, cramping, but I wouldn't break my stride.

When we reached the school, the winners were already in. As I crossed the finish line I could hear my heart in my ears. My ribs felt too small to hold my pounding heart, the air in my lungs. We were supposed to walk, stretch, and cool down slowly, but I lay in the bleachers, the sweat dripping into my ears.

I watched the clouds pass and the thick marine layer move over the field. The ocean air was moist and soft on my arms. My sweat dried, but the flush remained on my cheeks and my heart continued to pound. Had Owen's heart merely stopped, or had he waked up? Just before he died, did he wake, his heart pounding, like mine now at the end of a race? Maybe he stayed half-asleep, dreaming he was winning, out in front, or maybe he dreamt he was the very last boy to reach the finish line.

chapter three

When I got home that afternoon, my father was at work and Ruth listened to slow country music in their bedroom, the door shut. The soft twangs and low voices hummed over the electric buzz of the television. I didn't knock, but she knew I was home. She paid close attention to the noises of the house, and if she was waiting for my father to come home, she'd sit up, squinting, seconds before the garage door opened.

I showered with the bathroom door closed and the fan off, letting the room fill with steam. My cold fingertips tingled and burned as they warmed, and I breathed short breaths as the steam filled my lungs. When I got out of the shower, the skin on my chest and stomach was bright red. I loved hot showers, nearly burning. Like my mother, I was always cold, wearing sweaters in the summer and sitting in a hot car without rolling the windows down. Our condo was never warm enough. Trees behind it and the condominiums in front blocked the sunlight. The ceilings were tall and because of this we didn't use the central heating, but we heated each room with space heaters.

I had a large room. Our condominiums were built for roommates, college students who needed their own space. My dad and I each had a master bedroom, but mine had a balcony and a little vanity built into a wall with dressing room lights and deep drawers for makeup and hairbrushes. I didn't wear makeup except a pale pink lipstick at night, so the drawers sat empty, but the previous girl who lived in my room had left beige makeup smears and a bitter perfume smell in the bottom drawer.

I wanted to go to the party with Chloe and to feel people all around me happy and laughing. I wanted to put on nice clothes and look beautiful and sexy, but I was tired after the meet. So when the phone rang, I opened my door and listened down the stairs as Chloe left her message.

"I want you there, but you only have a half hour. Everybody's waiting," she said. They weren't waiting for me.

I knocked and called, "Ruth," through the door. I knocked again, and opened the door. She was asleep on top of the bed with the comforter wrapped around her. As I sat on the bed, the comforter opened around her shoulders. She was naked. Her shoulders were spotted with freckles and her chest was blotched and pink. I stood too quickly and she opened her eyes and pulled the comforter over her shoulders easily, as if I saw her naked all the time.

"What did you need, sweetie?" Her voice was hoarse and her eyes swollen.

"I was hungry and I wanted to know if you were too. I'd get us some food," I said.

"I'm not hungry, but you can get money from my purse and take my car," she said, and wiped at her face and hair. I put my hand on her hip, to warm it.

"Are you sick?" I asked.

"No," she said, and burrowed deeper into the blankets.

"Is Dad coming home?"

"He is, soon. He wants you to call him," she said. She took my hand from her hip and squeezed. Her fingers were hot and dry.

"I'll bring something back for you," I said, and she smiled.

"You take such good care of me." She put her hand back into the blanket and she closed her eyes before I stood. I turned off the television and the lights as I left, and she was asleep again before I closed the door.

I called my father on his mobile phone, but he didn't answer. My dad rarely picked up his phone and I didn't think he ever checked the messages.

"Dad, when you have a cell phone, it means you want people to be able to be in touch," I'd said one afternoon after trying him for hours.

"Kid, I'll always pick up for you."

I left a message for him. "Bring food home, or you'll find us gnawing our limbs off."

I pulled my jeans from the hamper and reached into my

pocket for the little paper ball that I'd fingered the whole school day. When I opened it, Farouk's writing had softened and smeared and the paper was fuzzy. It was rare that a boy would give me his phone number. Maybe those boys at the beach understood that I wouldn't want to call them because after that one night our kisses wouldn't be first kisses. I wouldn't feel my skin warm and grow goose bumps as soon as those fingers touched my stomach.

Katherine kept those shreds of napkin and half-used matchbooks in a jar next to her bed. She said she never called a boy, that if they wanted her they would call. The one time I was at her house, I shook it and tipped it over while she was in the bathroom, and some had shaky writing with numbers and a boy's name, but most were written in the same lightly looping hand.

Farouk's phone number was similar to mine; the first three numbers were the same prefix, while the last four were my own numbers mixed around. Maybe that number made it easier to pick up the phone. Maybe I expected that I'd be calling a home similar to my own, but mixed around a bit, comfortable because it was familiar and because it wasn't.

"Hello." He picked up without my end ringing.

"Hi," I said. He paused and I heard a door shutting.

"Samantha," he whispered into the phone.

"Can you talk?" I asked, pressing the receiver to my ear.

"No. Are you calling for tutoring?" he whispered again. He sounded like he couldn't get enough breath, as if he was crouching.

"I guess," I said.

"I'll meet you," he said. "Tell me where."

Why was he whispering?

"Hurry," he breathed. I heard a man calling his name in the background, and another extension in the house was picked up. Then I heard a whiny kind of music, with a woman singing in a different language, and I could tell from the steep drops in her voice that she sang about loss and sadness. Farouk held his breath and I wanted to speak, but I knew I had not called a house similar to my own. After a moment, the phone was hung up.

"Sam, where should I meet you?" he said in a normal voice.

"The Vons parking lot, off Mission Vista." I had been holding my breath, too.

"That's right by my house. I'll be there in fifteen minutes." He laughed and hung up. I kept the phone to my ear as the dial tone returned.

I took ten dollars from Ruth's bag and her car keys. She'd let me drive before, but if my dad was home when I asked to use her car, he'd tell me no before she had a chance to answer. It was a deep blue sports car, just a bit too nice for a teenager. When I turned it on the radio blared and I jumped. She listened to the same station I did and she drove fast. Once, we were on the freeway and she nodded to a man driving next to her, and he nodded back, so they raced, pulling between cars and twisting into open lanes.

"Don't tell your dad," she said, and we laughed.

That night, her car smelled like cherries and vanilla. I drove slowly, braking yards ahead of a turn. I'd never driven at night. Halos from the streetlights and headlights seemed closer than they were and then suddenly much farther away. I swerved to avoid a cat in the road, but as I looked again it was just shadows and beams from passing cars.

When I pulled into the lot, I felt breathless, like I had run there, my ribs tight over my heart. The market's lights cast a bright white glare and I found him under a streetlight, away from the cluster of cars near the entrance.

He leaned against an older white Jaguar. It had a dent in its side and a missing hubcap. I parked next to him and he leaned into my window.

"Not very much light here for studying." He smelled like pepper.

"I didn't know where else to go. You had me on the spot." I turned the car off.

"California kids have the nicest cars," he said, and opened my door, but stood in the way so I couldn't get out. He looked around me at the interior, the dashboard.

"Let's go for a ride."

"In your car?"

"Why don't I drive this one?"

"Okay." I'd be safer in Ruth's car, in control of where we went and what we did. I moved to the passenger's seat.

He got in, then opened the sunroof and drove west, toward the beach. He turned off the radio and drove without hesitation. He balanced the clutch and gas with both feet at lights, instead of putting it in neutral and pressing the brake. He drove like Ruth.

"I still get confused that west is the beach and east is the rest of the country." He turned on the heater and it blew hot on my chest and feet and the air from the sunroof cooled the top of my head.

"You seem to know your way," I said. We curved down and through the hills and a cluster of trees that kids called the enchanted forest. They drove into the fire trails to kiss and grow scared by the spindly trees and the ruts in the road and the sweet, choking smell of people burning the brakes down the hill.

"To the beach, and to the tidal pools. We used to go there when we were on vacation. I loved making the anemones swallow my fingers." He smiled at me, teeth white as oncoming headlights.

"I used to find starfish," I said. "They'd get stuck as the tide went out and my dad would throw them back into the waves."

At the bottom of the hill with the white cross on the top we could make a right to the beach, or a left up into the houses on the slope.

"Go left," I told him, because there were things I wanted to show him on the hill, things he'd have to know to fit in. "A lot of the kids from school drive up here; they have stories. I'll tell you the stories so you'll know when you make friends, find a crowd," I said.

"You won't be my friend, then?" he asked, his eyes on the traffic light. His arms were strong and he didn't flinch when a car ran a red. I felt safe with this boy, but I knew he could make me feel unsafe, terrified. I wanted to know that feeling too. I wanted to know what it was like to have him grab my upper arm, to feel his nails in the fleshy underneath. The sting and pull.

"I don't think so," I said.

He turned onto the hill and I gave him directions, though I hadn't been to Mount Soledad since I was eleven, a few months after my parents split up. My mother took me up the hill to watch the Blue Angels fly over the city.

"We'll be so close, we'll be able to see the pilots'

whiskers," she'd said. It was hot, summer. A jet flew over so close I could read the numbers on its belly and the noise made my heart change its beat. I must have jumped because my mom said, "I didn't know it would be so loud." She pressed me to her chest, her cool hands covering my hot ears as another jet passed. When there was a break, she held me to her hip and we ran to the car. Despite her hands on my ears, I lay in bed that night listening to the ringing in my head.

Now Farouk and I drove up toward the cross and he turned into a small winding street barely wide enough for two cars. There were no sidewalks and the houses were old with white shutters and dormer windows.

"These are the midget houses," I said. The lawns in front of the houses sloped down, but from the street the houses just looked short, the front doors two-thirds normal size. "The rumor is that all the munchkins moved here after they finished *The Wizard of Oz*," I said.

He slowed the car to look. Many houses had been rebuilt into modern homes with steep angles. They looked like they were crumbling into the hills. The midget houses looked fresh from the past, clean and innocent.

"Why La Jolla? Why would they move to La Jolla?" he asked.

"Because of the ocean views," I said, and he shook his head.

"You're supposed to tell me that if we sit too long the midgets will come out and hit the car with baseball bats. That way I'll squeal and jump closer to you," I said.

"I don't want to scare you," he said, and narrowed his eyes, smiling at me. My skin grew warm. He smiled at me for a second too long and my stomach fell like it did in the moment a strange boy would lean over, his breath in his throat, and kiss me.

He gunned the engine and we wound up the hill. I watched the ocean, and the faint line that separated the water from the sky. From the hill, the ocean looked calm, but I saw a whitecap, and another, and I knew different.

At the top of the hill we parked near the spiky black fence that surrounded the tall, white cross.

Outside the car my fingers grew numb and my hair felt wet. Farouk didn't stomp his feet, or clasp his hands together. He was warm.

"I've been here too, but never at night," he said.

"Your parents moved here to be on permanent vacation?" I asked. We sat on a bench and watched downtown San Diego, the harbor and the sailboats.

"No, but we did move into the condo we used for our vacations."

"And the car we drove up here is just my weekender," I said, and smiled. I wanted to laugh, to make sure he got my joke, to show him that I could make jokes. I could laugh and smile.

"We moved here because my father got into trouble with his company. He stole money, he settled the case and the condo was the only thing in my mother's name, so we were allowed to keep it." He looked me right in the eyes. His pupils and irises were a calm black like the ocean at night. I was still, afraid to stop smiling if he was still joking.

"You don't believe me?" he growled, pausing between each word. I stopped smiling and didn't move.

"I do, but it's a strange thing." My heart sped up again.

"I have the newspaper article," he said. "It names my dad. We left two weeks later. Why would I come into school after the start of a term, in the middle of a week?" He didn't raise his voice, but his hand was a fist in his lap. When he looked back to the marina, to the skyline, I watched that hand, his knuckles white.

After minutes, or maybe just seconds, he relaxed his hand and faced me again.

"You've been a good tour guide," he said. "I like the midget houses."

"You haven't seen the cross up close. It'll make you dizzy," I said, and stood. He followed me up the steps to the cross. I felt his warm body behind me and I wanted to stop short and feel him pressed against me, his arm around my waist as he steadied us.

We stood with our chests pressed against the fence. The metal was cold through my shirt as we looked up and I wanted to hold on to the posts to balance myself, but I didn't. My body wobbled and I laughed a scared gasping laugh, and it felt as though I would fall back and tumble down those steps and over the lip of the mountain and land with a small gurgle in the harbor with those tiny sailboats.

He jerked my shoulders and I screamed.

"You're too much," he said, leaving his hands on my shoulders. My breathing was shallow and my heart pounded from the adrenaline like it did in meets when I nearly passed a fast girl, a winner. And I thought I should kiss him. So I turned to him and leaned, my stomach doing an icy flip. He pulled back, but left his hands on my shoulders.

"You don't even like me," he said, and let me go, though he took my hand and led me down the stairs again. My hand felt small and cold in his, and I left it limp so he had to hold on tight. He led me back to the car and opened my door and closed it behind me like we were on a formal date.

We drove fast down a street with sharp curves with the sunroof open and the heater on high. We sped toward a stop sign. Cars crossed our path yards ahead and I felt free. I lifted my hands out of the sunroof, my fingers spread in the air, and I knew that if he drove me through that stop sign at forty miles an hour, I'd be safe, the cars would know we were coming. We'd make it through, clear, to the other side.

chapter four

I woke the next morning to music coming up through my floor: "Runaround Sue." My father woke me this way on weekends—by turning up the oldies station and singing along.

He was in the kitchen in his running shorts and a T-shirt. He didn't run at all for months, then ran ten miles a day for two weeks.

"Good morning," I said.

"Sam I am," he said, and put his arm around me. He smelled crisp like the outdoors and his shirt was wet from his run.

He pinched at his sides. "I feel fat. Kid, do I look fat?"

"No, Dad. Stop being such a girl."

He inhaled deeply and flexed his arms. "Do these look like girl arms?" he asked. His voice strained.

"They look like Mr. Universe's arms. I mean you should really enter contests. Weren't you on last month's cover of *All Brawn, No Brains*?"

He let his arms down and exhaled in a long whoosh. "Don't forget, you're the lucky one. You got the brawn *and* the brains. Brawn from me, brains from your mom."

Was that true? I looked like my father, deep clear blue eyes and a thin top lip with a full bottom lip. But Dad was smart. He helped me through *The Canterbury Tales* and *Macbeth.* Still, my mom was the brains. She was a history major in school and my dad often said that he passed college with her help. She read like some people slept, deeply, not able to be disturbed. She'd sit on the couch biting her cheek, her feet under the blanket on her lap.

"Mom," I'd say, and she wouldn't look up. "Mother." Her eyes still skimmed the page. I'd have to wait until she finished a chapter before she'd wake up from the book.

"Special breakfast this morning for my number one kid," Dad said, and let me go. He was slicing red onion and had arranged bagels and tomatoes and lox on a plate. This was not my favorite breakfast; it was his. He was born in Manhattan, in the Village, and though we weren't Jewish, he cooked like we were. This was a breakfast his mother made for him on weekend mornings.

"Grab the cream soda and have a seat," he said.

"Don't you think milk or juice would be a better breakfast for your only child?" I said.

"There's no dairy in cream soda?" he asked. "Does that mean there's no orange juice in Orange-Crush?"

"False advertising," I said, and took a sip. The fizz tickled and the cold soda tasted milky and delicious.

"Where's Ruth?" I asked. He brought out the plate and sat.

"Her stomach's pukey. And, Sam, please don't borrow her car anymore. You're not insured."

I took a bagel and spread cream cheese on a half. I salted the red onion and tomato and pressed it into the cream cheese.

"Why not put me on the insurance so I can drive?"

He put together his own bagel.

"Not yet. Too many kids get into accidents at your age. They have five of their friends in the car and they kill them all. The poor driver always seems to live. Could you go on with that on your shoulders?"

I wanted to argue, but I understood. I'd seen the yearbook photos on the news of kids who'd died in car accidents, kids who I could tell were popular or nerdy or sluts or invisible like I was. But even so, I wanted to make a deal to drive, like other kids did, based on grade improvement or chores, though there was nothing to clean around the house, we had no yard, and a housekeeper came once a week.

"You're right," I said. As I ate, I thought back on the night before, speeding toward the intersection and Farouk pressing the brakes at the last moment, the tires screeching and smoking as the car lurched, my palms smacking the rim of the roof, the seat belt snapping against my chest and digging into my ribs. I'd screamed. Cars honked and the black pickup truck in the intersection swerved. We stopped beyond the white line, beyond the stop sign, but Farouk acted like this was normal, waited his turn despite the honking and drove on, easy, like he had driven before.

When we returned to his car he handed me the keys.

"I must have missed the sign." He smiled, those white teeth glowing like the Cheshire cat's.

"Those bright red stop signs can sure be hard to spot," I'd said, still shaking.

I sipped at my cream soda now and it was so cold my head hurt and felt good at the same time.

"Ruth was sick last night too," I said. "Where were you?"

"I was working hard so that I could bring you breakfast this morning," he said, and smiled. The radio played "Brown-Eyed Girl" and I thought of Chloe. She said it was her song, though her eyes were hazel.

"Where were you?" he said, and tilted his head. He held his bagel up, ready to eat but waiting for my answer.

"With Chloe," I said, "and I'm not the one who should care for Ruth. I'm not her boyfriend."

"Samantha, I was at work. I'm not sure why you're doing this, but you could have stayed home and taken care of her. She takes care of you every day."

"Dad, I'm sixteen. She's not changing my diapers."

"She keeps you fed. She makes sure you've done your homework."

I took another sip of my soda. I needed a second because I wanted to yell. But I was afraid of making him mad. When we argued, he remained calm and then at a point I was always unable to detect, he turned and yelled and swore, and he hit me once when I wouldn't stop screaming back.

"Okay," I said. I finished my bagel. My dad ate slowly, so I waited for him.

"Any news on the boy's heart?"

For a moment I was nervous. What had he heard? Did he know more than I did?

"Not really. The cross-country teams were checked out and the doctor told us what to look for, shortness of breath, getting really tired after running. But that's how running is."

"Very true." As he finished eating, he looked up like I had said something, but his eyes traveled to a point behind me, just over my left shoulder. My time was up. He was thinking about work, or Ruth or another woman whom I would never meet. If I told him anything now, he'd forget or insist I'd never said anything at all.

After I washed dishes and my dad went to his room and shut the door, I changed into running clothes.

I'd just eaten, so I jogged very slowly. It was a warm morning and not many cars were on the street. I passed the parking lot where I'd met Farouk and I passed a park with balloons strung up in the trees. A group of people with dogs on leashes turned in circles.

I passed other condominium complexes and looked into the gated driveways, expecting Farouk's beaten-up white Jaguar. Despite the slow pace, my stomach cramped and I had to slow even more, until I walked, pressing my fingers into my stomach, and into my sides. I walked past the Mormon temple.

A bride stood with a bouquet, posing for pictures. Her dress was bright white, like the temple. The dress reflected onto her neck and face as she smiled. She shifted her shoulders and bent at the waist, her flowers hiding her cleavage, and the photographer took her photo. She was alone out there with him, flirting. She didn't look pure like the church. Perhaps she was like me, and had begun by flirting with boys, and wound up with their hot hands on her thighs, saying her name in a sweet, breathy whisper.

Dad was gone when I got back. No note. He'd be gone an hour or until evening; maybe he'd gone to have his car washed or to work. I couldn't imagine him going other places—he hadn't taken me to the beach in years and he rarely took Ruth to movies; he hated malls and the zoo. His circle seemed so small, but it was enough to keep him away from the house.

The blinds and my sliding door had been opened in my room. Dad often opened my window in hot weather and turned on my space heater in the winter.

I showered, then sat at my desk to begin my homework, an English paper on *An American Tragedy:* passion versus reason. I opened the book, and heard Ruth vomiting. The toilet flushed and I went into their room, my promise to my father echoing in my ears.

"Ruthie, do you need help? Do you want to go to the doctor?"

She slid under the blankets and lay on her side. She didn't look pale and sick. Her face was pink, her eyes bright, and her hair was full like she'd just finished styling it.

"I've been to the doctor, honey. I'm fine. I'll be back to normal in a minute," she said.

Why hadn't Dad told me she'd been to the doctor?

"What did the doctor say?"

She watched me, made a judgment. She was trying to keep her face relaxed but a brief shudder of her eyelid, a twitch she got when she was stressed or angry, gave her away. "He said it was nothing to worry about. Your father was there, if you want to ask him about it. I'm tired now, sweetie."

I went back to my room and sat in front of a blank sheet of paper, listening. Within an hour she was up and showered, moving around in their room. Turning on the TV and changing the channels fast before she could see what was on.

She opened their door. "I'm going out," she hollered.

"Where?" I said, standing up to go with her, but she was down the stairs and out the garage door. She normally invited me on errands. I sat and stared at my desk.

I was alone in the house. Ruth seemed to be here most of the time, cooking or cleaning. I went into their room and turned on the TV. She'd left it on a sports channel. It was an old football game, and the players had long, thick sideburns. The crowd cheered and the referee blew his whistle. I loved that sound.

I opened Dad's closet. He didn't have cool clothes for me to wear like dads who gave their daughters old flannel shirts or faded Levi's. My father's clothes were pressed plaid button-up shirts or khakis with creases down the legs. His jeans were a light blue, faded by the manufacturer. They smelled like him, a cinnamon, wood smell.

One of the teams scored a touchdown and the crowd yelled, fists in the air. A band played a fight song.

In their bathroom he kept a small basket full of his

change and I rifled through it for half-dollars though I didn't need money. I smelled his colognes and put on Ruth's too-red lipstick. It made my eyes fade and my skin pale.

Where did my father go all the time? Why did Ruth put up with it? Why didn't she tell him that his daughter wanted him home more?

I found Ruth's birth control pills. They were half taken, the empty plastic blisters creased and sharp under my thumb. The pharmacy label was stuck to the inside of the lid. The prescription had been issued three months ago and there were no full pill packs in her drawers. I took out a box of tampons and it was nearly full, the same one I had taken tampons from earlier in the month.

The phone rang and I jumped, dropping the box and tampons on the floor. On the television, football players fought each other, despite the referees' pulling them apart. The phone rang again and I ran to answer it, drawing a quick breath when I picked it up.

"Hello," I said, sounding nothing like normal.

"Samantha?"

"Hi, Chloe. I ran to pick up the phone. I'm glad it's you."

"What are you doing?"

"Homework."

"Oh." She cleared her throat.

"What's up?"

"Can I come over?"

"Of course. You don't need to ask," I said. "Bring your books. I have a paper due."

"I will," she said, and her voice trembled.

"Are you crying? What's going on?"

"I just need to get out of my house."

"Come over now," I said, and we hung up. I picked up the tampons and my hands shook. I tried to put them all back in the same direction, neatly. But no matter what I did, the box bulged.

chapter five

Chloe rang the doorbell in three short bursts. When I reached the door, she was out of breath, as if she'd run.

"Hi there," she said, cheerful despite her red eyes and the hoarseness in her voice.

"No one's home," I said, and we went up to my room. She dropped her books and folders in the middle of my floor.

"What's up?" I reached for her arm, knowing it would be hot under my touch and flushed pink from her cuts. She pulled at her long sleeves so they covered her fingertips.

"Let's go out on the balcony." We sat on the cold wood and she pulled a pack of cigarettes out of her sweatshirt. I'd never seen her smoke before. She lit a cigarette and handed it to me, then lit one for herself. I had only smoked a few times, but Chloe lit up smoothly, squinting.

"When did you start smoking?" I said.

"I know, they'll kill you and make your lungs black."

"That takes years." I held the cigarette between my fingers like she did.

She blew smoke out in a stream between us, then waved it away.

"Talk to me," I said.

"It's home stuff." She looked out into the condos.

Her parents were divorced. Her father lived right on the boardwalk in Pacific Beach and her mother had kept the big family house. Her mom was a grown-up version of Chloe, soft-looking and kind. She and Chloe often stayed up late into the night playing Monopoly.

"My brother's home," she said.

I inhaled a bit from my cigarette and blew it out without letting it into my lungs. Her brother wasn't around often. He lived in L.A. and didn't go to school. But sometimes he came back to San Diego and when he did Chloe wouldn't call me and sometimes she'd skip a day of school. When I asked her what he did in L.A., she said, "My dad pays for him to go to school, but I know he fails every semester." She didn't look at me and I knew I shouldn't have asked.

"I wasn't supposed to let him in," Chloe said, and exhaled smoke. "But he seemed okay. He had color in his face, and he'd gained weight." She stared into the condo across from us.

"You did what you thought was right," I said, and flicked the short ash of my cigarette.

"No, Sam, I did what I knew was wrong, and my brother stole from my mom."

When I looked up, she was squinting at me. My cheeks grew hot.

"He took her nice watch and her gold-coin ring my father had given her years ago."

I puffed again on my cigarette. My mouth was dry and my throat burned. "Can we get them back? Why don't we try to find him? Do you know where he hangs out?"

"This isn't an episode of *Scooby-Doo.* The stuff is gone. He sold it." I looked at her, but she watched the tip of her cigarette burn bright red as she blew on it.

"Do you want me to go and kick his ass? He's a total dick." I squinted too.

She leaned over and hugged me.

"I'm so sorry," she said, crying. She smelled like smoke and roses and her hair was cool on my face. I wanted to cry too, and tell her about Ruth.

"I feel so screwed up all the time," she said. "I'm a mess." She pulled back and wiped at her face.

"Having a messed-up brother doesn't make you messed up," I said. There were worse things that could happen to a family. I hoped that Ruth wouldn't remember how she left that tampon box months ago.

"We grew up together," she said. "The same things that happened to him happened to me."

She ground her cigarette against the side of the balcony. I copied her.

"You have no idea what happens to people when you're not around," I said. I wondered where Ruth had gone. Perhaps to the mall or to the beach to sit out without suntan lotion, which my dad warned her not to do. Maybe she was just driving fast up the coast watching the waves break white on the beach. And my father could have been anywhere, at another woman's house, or at his desk at work.

"No, I guess not," she said. "Where were you last night? The party was lame, but we could have walked someplace."

I pulled my knees up to my chest and I wanted to tell her, but it felt good to have Farouk as a secret. It was a small fire burning inside me, keeping me warm. If I told, there might not be enough warmth left.

"I was asleep last night. Tough meet," I said, and my voice was uneven from trying to act normal.

"Sam, our athlete. You'll have to help me get thin one of these days," she said, and lit another cigarette. She didn't offer me one.

"Whenever you want," I said, "but don't turn skinny on me. Have you noticed that half of those popular girls are so skinny they're bowlegged? No fat, no muscle."

"I doubt their legs are like that because they have fast metabolisms. Or even because they puke every time they eat a nut." She dragged on her cigarette.

"Are you saying the queens of the school are easy? Isn't that blasphemy?" I laughed. "Careful what you say, you might be struck down to the seventh circle of hell with the Dungeons & Dragons nerds."

"Some of those guys are cute," she said, and smiled so that her whole face lifted and brightened. "I like smart boys."

"Does smoking affect eyesight?" I grabbed for her cigarette.

"You know that your heart does a little dance when

you see them in the quad with their little silver wizards and goblins."

"I'm getting scared now. And cold. Let's go in."

I helped her up. I turned her hand over and there was a line of dried blood on her arm. It was thin, the length of a match. She pulled away.

"Chloe, please don't do this. It scares me."

"It scares me too."

"Next time you want to do that, call me instead."

"It isn't the same," she said, and opened the sliding glass door. The warm air blew toward me. The conversation was over.

She sat on the floor and leaned against my bed, opening her books. I sat at my desk and bit on a pencil.

"You know Owen's family never had a history of heart disease," said Chloe. She was drawing stars on her paper and didn't look up.

"How would I know that?" I asked.

She smiled at her paper. "My mom was telling me that she remembers Owen's grandma dying about ten years ago from cancer. And his other grandma came to the funeral. No heart trouble." Chloe stopped drawing and looked at me.

"Why would the doctor say all that? You can't make a doctor lie."

"Maybe they hadn't done an autopsy. I'm not the expert." She closed her notebook with a thud.

I heard the creak and pop of the garage door opening. When I stood, the blood rushed from my head, making me so dizzy I had to sit again.

"Is that your dad?" She opened her notebook.

"Could be," I said. Chloe continued to draw. I wasn't sure who I wanted to see more, Ruth or my father.

"Kid," he called. "Kid." He ran up the stairs two at a time and burst into my room carrying shopping bags.

"Hello, kids," he said. "Chloe, good to see you again."

"Same here," she said.

"Daughter, I've got some things for you here," he said, and left bags on my bed.

"Thanks," I said.

"Chloe, how are you? Studying hard?" he asked. "Are you staying for lunch?"

A wave of nausea hit me. "Dad, I think I ran too hard. I feel sick," I said.

"You're white." Chloe sat next to me and rubbed my back. "And cold."

Dad put his hand on my forehead. "Is it a migraine? Lie down." He got migraines too. When I had one, he'd sit with me and press a wet washcloth on my head. "I'm sorry," he'd say. "I know I passed them down to you."

"I'll leave then," Chloe said, and squeezed my hand. "Mr. Pallas, always a pleasure."

"Slice of heaven," said Dad, and bowed to her.

She felt my forehead. "I'll find my way out." But she lingered.

"I sorry." I felt bad. She didn't want to go home, to tell her mother about her stolen jewelry, or maybe she had more to tell me about Owen. And I wanted to hear more, but my head was aching, a small hole yawning open above my eyebrow.

"I'm sorry, Chloe," I said as she left.

"Feel better," she called from the stairs.

My dad took the bags off my bed and pulled my sheets

taut. I lay in bed and exhaled. He brought me a washcloth and pressed it to my forehead.

"What did you buy me?" I asked.

"Just some clothes," he said. He smiled at me and my heart broke. I loved him so much. And at that moment with his hand on my forehead, the good things he did outweighed the bad.

chapter six

When I woke it was dark. I found Dad downstairs at the table reading a days-old paper and Ruth cleaning the kitchen counters. It was quiet and dim in the house. I stood still, seeing how they were together when I wasn't around: quiet and separate. My father looked up and saw me on the stairs.

"Sam," he said in a loud voice like he was trying to warn Ruth that I might catch her doing something she shouldn't be.

"Dad," I said, and sat across from him. Ruth sat down and he put his hands flat on the table, palms pressing the glass top. He looked down, then at Ruth. She had a blank expression, watching from far away.

I could have saved him from this, by telling him I knew.

But I wanted to see this strange, small family collide with a big brick wall.

"Kid, Ruth is pregnant."

And I didn't have to try to look shocked. Hearing my father say it was shocking. Ruth was quiet. I felt a flush build from my chest to my neck to my ears.

"Congratulations," I said. And I saw us as we were, and the daughter, me, was a very sweet girl, caring and generous. And Ruth was poised and looked like a mother with her soft red hair and full body.

"I guess we'll need a bigger house," I said, and sat up straight. I was a very good person.

"We aren't moving," said my father. "We're not going to have the baby."

Ruth flinched.

"Why tell me?" I said, calm.

"We just wanted you to know that birth control can fail and that if you aren't ready for the results of sex, then you aren't ready for sex," he said, and stood. He pushed in his chair and turned around, finished.

"Well, this is a good way to teach me a lesson."

Ruth turned to me and smiled, her eyes tilted up at the corners. She was sexy, seductive the way my father preferred women to be. She smiled at me and I knew that I would help her.

"Sam," he said, "we all need to learn from this. If you want to be a brat, that's fine, that's what I'd expect."

He walked down the stairs and opened the door to the garage.

I felt slapped. I was a child, a brat.

"This was a shitty lesson for you," said Ruth. She stood and kissed my head.

"You'd be a good mother," I said.

"You'd be a great sister."

I wanted to believe her, but I was my father's daughter, not Ruth's.

Ruth pulled away from me and began straightening the place mats.

"It's a shitty lesson for you, too," I said to Ruth. She shook her head. I wasn't trying to be mean, just honest.

"Sam, why do you have to do that?" she asked, and went back to the kitchen. As she cleaned, I sat for a moment, alone in my cold house. And this was how it was on the other side of that brick wall, quiet, and calm like it was before.

I went back to my room and I called my mom. I let the phone ring until the machine picked up.

"Hey, Mom, it's me." I paused because it would make an interesting message for her when she got home. Dad knocked Ruth up. She's getting an abortion because Dad's a jerk. But it was too much to leave on her machine, so I took a deep breath. "Just missing you," I said. "I mean, I keep missing you. Call me when you can." I hung up and stood in front of my window without turning on the lights. I watched my neighbors. The college boy across the way had a lit candle next to his bed, but he slept. I sat and wondered what I would do if that candle caught his bedsheet on fire. Would I yell, run down my stairs and call the police, or would I sit here and watch and wait until someone else called the firemen, then watch as they hunted for his body?

chapter seven

I woke late on Monday morning and rushed to get ready. I gathered my books and the essay I'd written Sunday, locked in my room. I hadn't even left my desk when my dad knocked Sunday afternoon, interrupting my writing.

"Mom's on the phone," he called through the door.

I picked up the line.

"Hey, Mom."

"Hey, Sam. I've been missing you, too."

"How's Oakland? How's the lamp biz? Bringing light to people's lives?"

"Always," she said. She paused and I heard her take a

sip of something. Classical music played in the background. "What's going on?"

"Nothing." Another pause. There was shifting on her line and then a muffled whispering. Her hand was over the receiver.

"Mom?"

"Yeah, honey."

In the background I heard a man whisper, "Okay, okay."

"Is the TV on?"

"It is," she said.

"Okay, I was working when you called. An essay on *An American Tragedy*."

"They still make you read that book? Tell your teacher you want to read a book where a woman isn't killed. Tell her you'd like to read something about someone like you. A strong girl."

"I don't think those kinds of books are old enough to be on a high school reading list."

"Sure they are. Try *My Brilliant Career,* or *West with the Night.* I'm sorry, honey. It's just total crap," she said. She paused while she took another sip. I knew it was black tea with sugar and milk.

"I'll tell her, but for now I need to get back to this book."

"Is that it? Just writing an essay."

"It is."

"Okay. I love you."

"I love you."

I'd hung up, relieved.

On Monday morning, I threw on jeans and a sweatshirt and pulled my hair into a bun. When I came downstairs, Dad and Ruth had already left for work. They took separate cars and left a few minutes apart so they wouldn't arrive at the same time.

I cut between the condos. At the entrance to my complex I saw Farouk's car parked in the bike lane. I couldn't remember telling him where I lived. I walked toward the car. He leaned over the front seat and opened the passenger door.

"I thought I missed you. It's getting late," he said as I got in. He pulled away from the curb.

Despite the dents and the patches of rust on the outside, the dashboard was shiny with Armor All and the carpets had fresh marks from a vacuum.

"Why are you here?" I asked. His skin looked soft, freshly shaven, and his collar was pressed into a sharp crease. His nails were trimmed and clean and I wanted to touch his arm, to see if he felt as warm as he looked.

"I'm here to take you to school."

"What if I had taken my fast car?"

"A red-haired woman driving it passed me a while ago. She must have stolen it," he said.

"I'll call the cops later."

He'd sat there a long time waiting for me. I tried not to smile, but I couldn't help it so I turned to face the sidewalk as we drove.

"You would have been late if I hadn't been here."

"There are worse things to be," I said, though when I was late, my stomach ached from nerves and the embarrassment of walking into the classroom after the teacher had begun. The moment everyone looked up at me, I wanted to fall through the floor, though they probably thought nothing.

"Many worse things," he said. He drove with his hand at the bottom of the steering wheel and turned on the radio with his other hand. He had it programmed to a jazz station. Static crackled just below the music. It was the old jazz, sung to be sad, or desperate, not like the new jazz meant to be synced up to laser displays. And with that old music playing and Farouk driving, I felt like I could drive with him forever, out of San Diego, to the middle of nowhere and then back again.

But he got into line behind the other cars pulling into the school's lot. Once again I was smiling too much so I turned away. He parked in the teachers' lot, far from the other students.

"You can't park here," I said.

"They have no way to know which car is a teacher's and which is mine," he said. "Relax a little."

"Just trying to help," I said, and slammed the door, but it felt good to take a spot from one of the teachers.

We walked into school, and as I passed the trophy case I noticed a large photo of Owen. He wore his tracksuit and his face was shiny with sweat. Though he had no ribbon, I could tell from his smile and the relief in his face that he had just won a meet. The photo was poster-sized. On the floor below people had left flowers and stuffed animals and candles.

"Poor kid," said Farouk. He kissed my cheek and turned toward his classroom.

I looked around, but no one had seen him kiss me. They were looking at the Owen memorial, with their heads down.

I spent homeroom replaying that moment with Farouk, feeling that small fire inside me flare each time I thought about the way he leaned to me, his breath on my skin, finally touching me in the halls in front of all our classmates.

I was already sitting when he came into math class. "Sam, hello," he said loudly as he took the seat next to mine.

"Hello, Farouk," I said. The blond surfer girl behind me put her feet on the bookrack under my chair and rocked me forward and back.

The teacher began class, but I felt Farouk's dark eyes on my shoulders and on the bare part of my neck. The girl pressed her feet into my chair and my desk lunged forward. My neck burned. I wrote numbers from the board on my paper, but as I rocked and compared my notes to the board, the figures seemed to shift and shake and fall off the page.

"Sam, do you understand what's going on?" Farouk whispered to me.

"Yes."

"It doesn't look like it."

I covered my notes with my hand, but the numbers spilled over the sides.

"I'm fine," I said in a normal voice, and the teacher turned and looked at me, then at Farouk watching me. She turned back to the board.

And I breathed again. I put my feet on the floor and pushed back as the blond girl shoved me forward. I steadied myself and the numbers, but I didn't take another note. I let the lesson pass right by.

After history, I found Chloe waiting outside my class. She must have left early to have made it to my door before we were let out.

"Ready for lunch?" she said.

"I am. What's up?"

"Little bit of this, little bit of that," she said, and I smelled cigarettes in her hair and her clothes. "More Steinbeck. Biblical metaphors, dust, floods, whatnot."

She walked one step ahead of me, and opened a fire door. The sunlight stung my eyes, and the world was at once dark and light as the warm, dry wind pushed papers and tissues through the parking lot. A Santa Ana was blowing, making windows pulse and shudder.

"Did the new kid read again?" I asked. I was glad that she was still ahead of me because a blush moved up my neck and into my face.

"I can't remember," she said.

"Are you all right?"

"Are you?" She turned around. I took off my sweatshirt because I needed a moment to compose myself.

"I'm just hot. The Santa Anas make my nose bleed." I wanted to tell her about Ruth, but I was afraid of the way she stood in front of me, her arms crossed, blocking my way. She would not let me go until I told her all the things that made her suspect me of being secretive.

"I fought with my dad yesterday. He thought I wasn't being nice to Ruth," I said. Most of it was true.

"That's all?"

"That's it."

She held my gaze. "I guess you'll tell me when you're ready," she said.

She might have understood. Her brother was probably on drugs, heroin maybe. But at that moment a brother who shot up drugs and stole from his mother seemed more normal than a father who gets his girlfriend pregnant. California kids did drugs. But my own father's situation was the problem of a high school boy, not the problem of a man who should know better. A man who owned a corporation and had a daughter to look after, to make sure she didn't get pregnant and to lead her to live a happier life than his.

But Chloe was waiting for me to tell her everything that was on my mind, to be a friend to her by letting her be a friend to me.

"I'm fine, I'm well."

"Me too."

"Aren't you warm?" I said, because I wanted to press her, and not let her walk away, so she would know how it felt. "Are your arms okay? It's hot out." I wanted to see the pale pink scars and the fresh burgundy cuts. "I told you to call me if you were going to hurt yourself."

"The heat feels good," she said, and walked away from me.

I followed as she zigzagged between parked cars and didn't stop as she crossed a moving car's path. I let the zipper from my sweatshirt drag along the car doors as I walked. The kids at my school had fast new cars, red or black, cars that looked like a newspaper headline waiting to happen.

"Where are we going?" I asked.

"Off campus."

"I'm hungry."

"You'll be back in time to grab something on the way to class."

We left the school grounds and walked up the hill toward my house, but Chloe stopped just beyond the school, where Owen had stopped me that day on the trail. She turned into the canyon and I followed slowly.

She walked under the bridge and cars rumbled from the

street above. She sat as high as she could go on the canyon floor without her head hitting the bottom of the bridge. I stood as close as I could get to her, but I didn't want to sit. Graffiti surrounded her where she sat on the ground, behind her and on the underside of the bridge. Some was done in spray paint with angular letters, and tag names I couldn't read. And some clear in Magic Marker.

Boys had written their names, and a girl's name and a date. Some of the writing was faded, with dates from years ago, and some of it was just a month old. Scraps of trash covered the ground and in the shrubs I could see the bright blue corners or gold foil coins of condom wrappers.

"Just sit down," said Chloe. "Nothing will get you." She patted a place next to her. The cement looked clean so I crouched down and wedged myself between her and the bridge. I touched the cement over my head. It vibrated even when no cars were passing over us. Next to my hand was a girl's writing. She'd written in pencil, the lines shaky as the lead passed over the bumps in the cement. *Tami and Erin's dream disappear machine.* I didn't know a Tami or an Erin. What was a dream disappear machine? Were they like Chloe and me, girls who had secrets they couldn't even tell each other? Or were they happy girls, best friends, who thought those words would be funny, who laughed as they wrote them, picturing a girl reading them months or years later and pulling her hand away as if she'd been burned by such a scary-strange idea under a rumbling bridge.

"Why are we here?" I asked.

"I was just tired of being around people," she said.

"Did your mom notice her jewelry missing?"

"My brother came back when she was there. I think

he returned it. He acted like a normal person, and he and my mother had a nice conversation." She lit a cigarette. The smoke surrounded me, and I worried that my lungs wouldn't hold as much air during practice, but I didn't wave it away.

"That's good," I said, though it didn't seem likely that he would return things he'd stolen.

"My mom is letting him stay for a few days," she said, and took a drag on her cigarette.

"It sounds like your brother is really making an effort."

"It's bullshit," she said. I knew it too, but I shook my head like I thought I should.

A wind blew up through the canyon. Dust bloomed around us and I felt it settle on my skin. I coughed and turned my head away, and as I did, I saw Owen's name and date just weeks earlier, and *Samantha.* It was strange that Owen had been here with a girl named Samantha, because I was one of only two at my school. Why would he have been down here with the other Samantha, a quiet girl on the honors track to valedictorian? And then I gasped. He meant me.

"What's wrong?" said Chloe.

"I thought I saw a snake," I said, "but it was nothing."

The bridge above us shook as a bus or a truck passed overhead. Chloe leaned over me to look before I could block her or cover the marks. I smelled her clean hair.

"Did you know him from cross-country?" She leaned back.

"I didn't know him at all," I said. My voice broke and I heard myself as Chloe must have heard me, like a liar.

"But you were on the team together, right?"

"Yes."

"Why would you come down here with him?"

"I wouldn't. I didn't. I've never been down here before, with anyone."

"Get me a rock," she said. I found a stone and handed it to her. She began rubbing the place, but the rock just made thin, uneven scratches. She rubbed for a minute and looked up at me. Her face was flushed.

"You get a rock too," she said, and I knelt across from her and we scrubbed at the rough cement, but the writing would not disappear.

The *a*s in my name were large ovals, the *s* a soft curve. Each letter was a perfect copy of a handwriting text, and for a moment I was touched that Owen had written my name with a careful hand. Chloe's rock knocked into mine, pinching the tip of my finger, but she didn't stop. And so I continued to rub despite the lovely writing made by a dead boy. What if his parents hadn't kept anything he'd written, or the things they kept were written when he was a child, or when he was older but in a rush? They would never again see the lovely writing.

Chloe pulled up her sleeves and continued to rub, her nails becoming jagged and split. As she rubbed I saw the marks on her arm, thin lines across her skin, the translucent white scars and some pink. Two were fresh.

I touched one.

"Why do you do it?"

"It's like running," she said. She was breathing hard. "I never told you, but one afternoon I went running. I wasn't good. Not like you, but I ran as far as I could and a little bit farther. My legs felt like noodles and I thought I'd die on the spot, but I also felt great, like I was floating. It feels the same as when I cut."

"Oh, Chloe. Why don't you run with me, then?"

"I'll never be as good as you are. I'll just make you bad."

"How can you know that? Everyone gets better. Each time you run farther and faster. I'd help. It'd be better than this."

"It's not like I'm really hurting myself. I'm not trying to kill myself."

"How can I know that?" I held her wrist tight. She dropped the rock.

"You have to trust me," she said.

"I do. But I'm not a good friend if I let you hurt yourself." She looked at me, her eyebrows pressed together, making deep lines in her forehead.

"It's okay," I said. Tears began to float in her eyes.

"We need to get back." She sat on her heels. Her hair was touching the bridge and the cars hummed over us. She looked at her arm and slowly pulled her sleeve down. She squinted at me. "Did you sleep with him?"

"I never even kissed him. He asked me to come down here and run the trails; he offered me a ride home. I knew he didn't want to run so I told him no."

"I would have come down here with him."

"No, you wouldn't have. He thought he could get any girl."

"He could have." She scooted on her butt to a place where she could stand. The writing was smudged and dirty-looking and as I moved away I saw that now it drew attention to itself. Now it was something someone had tried to cross out, something secret, though the writing itself was still clear.

"He was such a jerk. He was mean." I inched down the hill.

"All those guys are mean. That's how you become popular. That's how you get people to love you. We'll never be good at it," she said. When I reached her she held her hand out. I took it as we walked back over the slope of the canyon and into the street. Despite everything, with Chloe's hand in mine and the warm sun on my skin and the dry air pulling my skin tight, I felt a surge of love in my heart and a lightness in my chest for the possibility of it all.

I ditched my first practice later that week. Farouk found me alone in a classroom, gathering my books after the end of class. The teacher had stepped outside and the room was quiet and dark.

When the door opened, the light was bright around the dark shape of the teacher. The classrooms had no windows because the canyon the school sat in was a fault line.

"I'm almost finished," I said, stuffing books into my bag.

The shape moved toward me. "We have time."

Farouk. I became alert in the dark room. He touched my arm, his fingers warm through the light cotton of my shirt.

"I'm taking you to the beach this afternoon," he said. "Meet me in the parking lot."

"I have practice."

"They won't miss you this one time," he said, and leaned into me. He ran his fingers down my hand.

"I'll miss it."

"Just once, no more. I'll run with you on the beach if

you're going to be upset. Come on." Farouk pressed his thumb into my collarbone. And then moved up from the bone into the groove between the bone and my shoulder where water sometimes collected while I showered.

I looked up at the small square of glass in the door and I wished someone was there looking in at us, a handsome boy touching his girlfriend, the girl with her head bent, long hair falling over her face. We could have been Owen and Linda. Two people very much in love.

"Okay," I said. "Okay."

"Meet me at my car," he said, and walked out.

All through my last class, I thought of excuses for Coach. My stomach began hurting as the end of the day neared. Now I wouldn't have to lie.

Coach Rose tried to make her tiny office welcoming with cut flowers and posters of women athletes—basketball players, boxers, surfers. There were no photos of ice skaters and gymnasts because those were sports women had always dominated. She wanted to show us women who were strong enough to fight for their sport, that she believed that each of us could be or would be those women, including me.

I leaned against her door. "I don't feel well," I said before she looked up.

"Hey, Sam," she said, startled.

I touched my stomach like I'd seen Ruth do.

"Do you need a doctor?" She stood. I backed up. If she touched me she'd know I was lying.

"Is it your chest? Do you have shortness of breath?" She was thinking of Owen. Maybe he'd gone to his coach with a similar feeling.

"No, I just didn't eat enough today. I get nauseated when I don't eat enough."

"Okay, sweetie. You had me worried."

She touched my elbow and looked at me with those blue eyes, never doubting me. I wanted to cry.

"Will you be all right? Did you call your folks to get you?"

"No, my friend is taking me home. She's waiting at her car," I said.

"All right. Call if you need anything." She went back to her desk. I believed it all myself until I walked out in the bright sun and found Farouk leaning against his car, squinting from the sun. For a moment I wished it really was Chloe taking me home and taking care of me, not this stranger who had no idea how to keep me safe.

"Did they cry and beg you to stay?" He took my backpack.

"They worry that one of us will be another Owen," I said.

"That heart stuff about Owen is bullshit. I asked my dad, and he said the chances of that happening are so small. One in a million."

He put my bag in the trunk and my body felt light without the weight. The line of cars had filed out, and I was alone with Farouk.

"One in a million means it has to happen to someone. Why couldn't it be Owen?"

He opened my door and stood waiting for me to get in.

"I understand that Californians think they live in the center of the world, but they don't. Your school isn't magical. Owen isn't any more special than any other prom-king jock anywhere else."

"I don't have to go with you," I said. "And you can just go home and stare at your walls and think about how unmagical everything in California is."

He shook his head and smiled. He left the door open and walked back to me. He leaned over to my ear. "Get in the car. I'll show you some magic."

He took the freeway west, toward the beach, and didn't ask for directions. I thought of the magical places he might take me, but there was just the beach.

Farouk parked at the beginning of the tourist strip in La Jolla.

I followed him between bushes and down a muddy path that bordered a drop-off into shrubs. The ocean boiled far below, churning over sharp rocks, and beat into the cliffs. Farouk walked with confidence, stepping over deep holes in the path and skirting muddy patches. I took a deep breath as I stepped in his footprints. My sneakers felt slippery and I couldn't tell if my feet were really jerking beneath me or if I imagined what it would take for me to fall over the edge.

We passed a couple walking away from where we were going. The knees of her pants were muddy and torn and the skin there was pink with small smears of blood. She walked ahead of the boy, pulling his hand. She didn't look down as she stepped, as if she thought falling once was enough. But I knew different. It wasn't like chicken pox; she could keep falling and scraping her knees until she learned that she must step carefully over the snake holes and muddy patches.

The grass grew tall, and beyond that houses stood, their

tall windows reflecting the cloudless sky, turning the blue warped and gray.

We made a sharp turn and a large rock jutted up from the ocean. A narrow bridge of rock joined our path to this rock. Farouk paused, waiting for me to catch up. He took my hand and began to walk over the bridge. I let go and pulled my fingers through his.

"This way, Sam."

The bridge was wet from bare feet walking over it and water dripped over the edge into the sea far below. It seemed too narrow for both my feet, but too wide for me to hold on to if I fell.

"One step and you're over," he said.

"I can see the rock from here. Yes, it is very amazing how water and nature have carved it out of the cliff. Wonderful, really."

"This isn't what I wanted you to see. One step, Sam. I'll hold on to you," he said. He let go of my hand and stepped onto the bridge and then over onto the rock. He was safe. He stepped back to me, then stood in the middle.

"People do it all day every day. If someone had fallen, this wouldn't be open."

A wave broke on the rock and the mist felt cool on my face. In one movement his arm reached behind my knees, his other arm behind my back, and he lifted me. He was as strong as he looked. For that second he carried me over the water I heard my heartbeat in my ears like I'd been running. My muscles were tense so that I wouldn't be too heavy, and yet ready to move with him if he lost his balance.

On the other side he put me down.

"Nothing to worry about," he said, and walked away

from me to the edge of the rock. Standing alone there was magical, though I knew this wasn't what he meant. Mist settled on me even when waves weren't surrounding the rock and breaking all around me.

Farouk disappeared over the side. I knew he wouldn't leave me here to find my way back over that small stretch to the rest of the world. I walked to where I'd last seen him and beneath me there were steps onto a lower level of the rock, where Farouk stood talking with other men whose swimsuits dripped water onto the brown dirt, turning it red. Their skin was brown, with goose bumps covering their arms and chests. Farouk looked out of place in his slacks and loafers.

A set of waves began to roll in. From the rock it looked like little ridges in the water, but I knew those ridges would turn into waves as they came near the shore and the sand rose up halfway as deep as the water. The sets came close and Farouk stepped aside. A man pressed his back against the rock beneath me. If I'd thought about what he was going to do I would have knelt down and grabbed his shoulder. He ran to the edge and jumped.

I gasped.

Farouk turned to me. "See how he hung there for a second?" The falling man lifted his feet behind him and grabbed his toes and for a moment he was still in the air, stopped between falling and floating away, and then he dropped out of sight and into the water. Like magic.

Farouk peered over the edge at the man swimming back to the rock. Then he stood below me and looked up, his hands at my feet on the dirt.

"Would you do it?" he said. I knelt down to him, my knees on the hard dirt, small stones digging into my skin through my jeans. I pressed my palms into the tops of his hands and he smiled at me. My shirt fell loose in the front and if he'd wanted to he could have looked and I would not have minded. I would not think he was taking advantage or being a typical boy. I wanted him to see me, to look at my body so that I could become real to him. And I wanted to feel the warmth from his skin so I could understand that he was a separate body that I could only press into so far.

"I would," I said, not because I knew he wanted me to, and not because I wanted to plunge into the cold dark water. I would just because for one moment I would know that it was possible for gravity to give up its hold on me, that maybe if I wished hard enough I could make my body rise up and float and mimic what I felt in my heart.

"I would too," he said, and I hoped his reasons were like mine. Another man jumped and Farouk watched my eyes and I leaned over and kissed his neck. My lips felt cool on his skin and I kissed him because I believed that he too wanted what I wanted, peace and focus and a little bit of quiet.

"Come down here," he said, and he held my hand as I leapt. We were able to sit on the ground and leave enough room for the others.

"This jump is easy. They just have to jump beyond the rock; they don't have to clear anything."

"Just the rocks beneath," I said.

"That's why they wait until high tide."

Each time a man ran and leapt off the edge Farouk would lean forward, his arm on my knee.

What if the diver had planned it wrong and the rocks were closer than he'd anticipated and he did not come up for air? Would the other men dive in immediately, despite the danger, or would they wait for the next set? Would Farouk go in after them or would he hold me, blocking my eyes and taking me away?

We sat until our backs hurt and the sun turned from a butter yellow to orange. I could have stayed forever watching those men hang in the air.

I was drowsy, leaning against Farouk, when he pulled away from me and stood. "Let's go." He didn't offer me his hand. I stood, blood rushing into my ankles and feet, making them feel swollen. Farouk put his feet into the small ledges in the rock to get to the first level, and I followed, my heels wobbling outside the holes. He was at the bridge before I was completely over the rock. He looked back at me once, then walked over to the path.

I waited for him to help me again, but he stood on the other side watching. "Sam, please hurry."

I put one foot on the bridge, and looked down at the white water beneath me. It was calm, just a froth rolling around on the rocks. If I fell, the water looked deep enough to catch me and lift me back again safe. But I knew there were rocks under the water that I wouldn't see until just seconds before I hit.

"Sam, lift your other foot and walk," he said, and began to walk away. I held my breath and lifted my foot and stepped over the water beneath me and onto the path.

He turned the heat on in the car and it smelled dusty and warm.

"Thank you for taking me out," I said as we pulled away.

He cut off a car and turned left without yielding. "I'm late. I'm supposed to be studying."

"Why? You seem to know it all."

He raced up a hill. The car vibrated under my feet.

"This school is too easy. My dad expects me to study things outside of school so I can keep up."

"Keep up with what?" I asked.

"I'm going to be a doctor. All of the men in our family are doctors. Our family were doctors to the shah of Iran," he said. I didn't know who the shah of Iran was, but I was jealous. I wanted to know important people, to have a legacy that I needed to live up to.

"I'm going to be a Dallas Cowboys cheerleader," I said, and smiled. He didn't look away from the road and he didn't smile.

"Excellent, Samantha."

"Joking," I said, and he waited for me to tell him what I was really planning to be. But I had no plans. If I was lucky a local school would accept me onto their track team and I'd run and take classes until I found something I was good at.

"You could grow your hair and cut it every year and make a beautiful wig. Sell it for a ton of money, then start all over again," he said, and looked at me for the first time in minutes, as if he knew that I was trying to think of something important I could spend my life doing.

"I could become a running-shoe tester."

"You could run a kissing booth," he said, and smiled at the road, but his hands were still tight on the wheel. I could have chased him for months or years. Maybe that would be my calling.

"You don't know whether my kisses are worth money," I said. I was relaxed. I was with a boy in a car on the way home from the beach.

I directed him through the maze of condominiums to my door, hoping he'd remember the turns and the dead ends so he could come back for me.

He pulled over and kept the engine on and his hands on the wheel. Still, I sat watching him. He would have to kick me out, or tell me that he was worried about his father finding him in his car with a strange girl with sand on her shoes.

"I like it when you drive me."

"I like driving you," he said. He spread his hands on the steering wheel and looked at his nails, clean and bright against his skin.

"Driving me crazy," I said. "Kidding."

His hands dropped from the wheel and he turned to me. He raised his hands and pushed them under my hair, onto my neck. His fingers were just cool enough for me to feel him press, slightly, then let go.

He leaned toward me and widened his eyes. He was scared, but he kissed me with his mouth closed. He left a small, cool wet spot on my lips that tasted metallic.

"I'll see you later," he said. "I have to go."

I'm sure I looked normal as I climbed out. But my skin felt swollen and hot.

The lights in the kitchen and my father's bedroom were on. I unlocked the door and heard the water in the kitchen turn off. Clothes were spinning in the washer.

"Hello," Ruth called.

"Hello." My voice was normal in my ears. And my house looked the same, the same white walls and the popcorn ceiling. And there was Ruth in her baggy clothes cooking dinner with a dish towel over her shoulder. "Kids drive Jaguars these days?"

I stopped. I should have had him drop me off on the other side of the condos. We had gone right by the kitchen window.

"It's an old one, with dents," I said.

"Who is he?"

"He's a new kid. He's in my math class. He's helped with my homework," I said.

Ruth paused and looked at me. She touched the towel, and dropped one hand to her stomach. I knew I was smiling. With Ruth, I couldn't turn away or hide it with my hand. She'd seen it already.

"Your cheeks are pink. Do you have a fever?" Ruth smiled at me. She rubbed her belly. It didn't look different, but I knew she felt something.

"I must," I said. Heat rose from my shoulders and neck. I let Ruth smile and watch me blushing. I was ready to laugh at myself, at Farouk for being nearly terrified to kiss me, and at Ruth for mimicking my silly smile.

"Bring him by for dinner. Your dad will want to meet him," she said. She turned back to the kitchen. I touched my lips as I watched her move. Her hips looked wider; her body was changing. Or maybe I was wishing it to.

I walked up to my room and dropped my things. The phone rang and I jumped and answered before the first ring ended.

"Hi, kid."

"Hi, Dad."

"Listen, I need your help. Could you tell Ruth that I'm going to dinner with the programmers and that I won't be home until late?" he said. But I heard voices and music and glasses clinking. He was already at dinner.

"Why can't you tell her? Why does this require my help?"

"Because you picked up the phone, and you're more convincing about things than I am."

I paused. In a self-defense class that I took with Ruth, the teacher said, "One way to discourage threatening phone calls is to blow a whistle into the phone." If I'd had a whistle I would have blown it into my father's ear.

Or I could have told him that he was a jerk for this and that Ruth deserved better. And that he could do better. He could love her like he loved me. But he'd be mad if I argued with him. If I yelled, Ruth would hear and know that my dad was hurting her.

"I hope I meet a man just like you when I grow up," I said. He laughed the way I hated, the way he did when we fought and he was finished arguing. He laughed like that to let me know that I'd lost.

"Love you, kid. And thanks."

I hung up after I'd waited a second, listening to the buzz on the empty line.

I stood at the top of the stairs and called down to Ruth, "Dad's having dinner with the programmers from work. He'll be home later."

I could picture her down there. She didn't rinse her hands under the faucet and she didn't open the cupboard for spices. I don't think she even took a step. I didn't move from the landing and she didn't move and I waited for her to come out of it and continue. She clicked a burner off and moved a pot and I breathed again.

I touched my palms to my toes with a flat back like the coach insisted and the stairs looked so steep that I felt close to tumbling down them, like my childhood dreams in which I tumbled down escalators and stairways without ever reaching the bottom.

Ruth had made paella for dinner and there was much too much even if my father had been there. She would expect me to take it for lunch and eat it as a snack when I came home from cross-country. I had a hard time with the prickly shrimps with their heads still on and the lumpy sausage buried in bites.

"How was practice?" she asked.

I looked closely at a bite, pretending to examine a clump of rice. I hadn't thought of Ruth asking me questions, about having to lie to her.

"My coach was sick," I said with my face close to the plate.

"Well, everyone's body needs a break. If she's sick again, you can come home early and help around here."

"Sounds good. I'll come home right after school."

I didn't mind helping, and would have cleaned more than I did, but Ruth told me she enjoyed it. She said cleaning helped her gain order in her mind.

She ate in small bites, and I saw that she too pushed the shrimp away and sausage gathered in a little pile on her plate.

"I guess I overextended myself on this dinner," she said, and smiled at me.

"Even the best chefs make mistakes."

For a moment the room felt soft, and warm and safe.

"When do you go to the doctor?" I pressed my yellow rice flat on my plate.

"I went today."

I dropped my fork and looked up. "You seem okay." In sex ed they'd discussed abortions and said women were often sick after and in pain. "You didn't have to cook. I feel terrible. I had no idea."

"It's okay. I went to an ob-gyn. She said I was too far along. I'm into my second trimester." And she laughed, at first quietly, and then with long deep laughs. She threw her hands in the air and laughed.

And so did I. I laughed until my stomach burned and I couldn't catch my breath.

"It's not funny," she said, out of breath, but still smiling.

"I guess not," I said. We started up again. I laughed because I pictured my father's face when he heard the news and I laughed from the pure joy of seeing Ruth, beautiful Ruth, getting exactly what she wanted.

I heard the first rumor in the bathroom as I washed my hands. Two senior girls talked through the stall door.

One girl leaned against the door and stared at herself in the mirror. She didn't stop looking at herself when I walked in front of her to get a paper towel. "You know one of the side effects of steroids is heart trouble," she said. She turned to the side and sucked in her stomach and put one hand on her stomach and one on her back.

"My mom said the same thing," said the girl in the stall.

"Well, I wouldn't put it past him. There's no way that guy could have been on that many teams and not have gotten some help." And the girl relaxed her stomach and rubbed her hips as if that might smooth the slight bulges.

"And he would need to be strong to fight off Linda's homies in the hood," said the girl in the stall. She flushed. I pulled my fingers through my hair, acting like I wasn't eavesdropping. But those girls didn't notice me and even if they had, I'm sure they would have been happy that they were the first to spread that information.

At lunch Chloe lay on the lawn. Her legs were stretched in front of her and she leaned on her elbows, watching our school.

"Hey, you," she said to me over her sunglasses.

I sat next to her and crossed my legs.

Chloe spoke without taking her eyes off the people in the quad. "Since first period I've heard that Owen was on steroids, that he was killed in a gang shoot-out and that he's not dead at all but his dad kicked him out for good."

"I just heard that he was on steroids."

"That's old news," she said. "These kids don't know anything. His family was messed up." She sat up. "I would have killed myself too if I had to live in that house."

I looked at her. "You never told me that. They'd have to be pretty messed up for him to kill himself," I said.

"If you knew them, you'd understand." She put her sunglasses on again.

"All of our families are messed up," I said. "He was a great runner. I can't see him killing himself."

"Maybe he didn't love it like you do. Maybe he just did it to make his dad proud. Maybe he really hated it."

"He was the best on the team, and you can't be that way if you hate it." But even as I said it, I began to doubt. Maybe love had nothing to do with it. I loved running as much as the girls who won, but I still spent each meet in the middle of the pack when I should be out in front, running hard, setting the pace for the others.

"Maybe he knew it was the best he'd be at anything. Ever. And that wasn't enough."

I put my head on my knees. Was I like Owen? Maybe all I'd ever be was a middle girl. Maybe it was time I tried to be better at something else.

chapter eight

I'd intended to ditch just the one time, but it became easier to give Coach an excuse. The next time I told her I had a migraine, and then the time after that Farouk forged a note for me from my mother saying I had a family obligation. Coach Rose was concerned. She asked me to please see a doctor or she would find one for me. In the beginning she was very trusting, and I soon stopped feeling bad about what I was doing. I was still running at home on the weekends, and in the afternoons if Farouk had to be home earlier than usual and Ruth wasn't home, I'd change into my running clothes and run around my neighborhood.

During the practices I went to, it seemed that not running made me stronger, and my body stored energy that I used on the hills. I ran fast and strong, my breath even and my hearing sharp and clear. I trailed those fast girls so close, I smelled their clean sweat. I didn't pass, though I'm sure I could have. I was no longer concerned with catching them. Instead I would think of Farouk as I ran. I thought about how he'd whisper in my ear that he wanted me with him, that he wanted to be alone with me, to pull his fingers through my hair and watch the surfers.

And when I was at practice Coach told me she was impressed by my improvement, that she could see that I was focused, my energy was clear and calm. I wouldn't tell her there was a boy who made me calm and made me scared and sometimes held my wrist so tight that my fingers tingled.

"You'll win soon," she said as I stretched after a run through the canyon where Chloe and I had found Owen's name paired with mine.

And as I improved she minded less that I was gone more afternoons. She would look up at me as I made up some new excuse. She'd tilt her head and look at me, and then at her posters and back at me. "Okay."

Farouk and I went to La Jolla Shores and to Marine Street, where Chloe and I had looked for the surfer boys with tattoos and orange surfboards the color of a 50-50 ice cream bar. He took me to new beaches, south to Dog Beach where dogs ran off their leashes. At that beach the homeless men sat in circles in the sand and laughed, passing a joint between them. And girls in long skirts and bare feet and ankle bracelets picked their way along the sand watching for broken glass or shells that could cut their feet, and for small toys they could tie to their braids.

We went north to a beach called Swamis, because of the gold domes and white spires of the secret religious center that bordered the parking lot. White light fixtures shaped like turbans marked the wooden staircase to the beach. The steps were fraying and the bolts holding them together were orange from rust. Wet marks traveled up and down the stairs from the surfers' feet. When the tide was out the sand stretched for more than a quarter of a mile and as we walked the mussels on the exposed rocks pulled and popped water as they siphoned it and made bubbles with their sharp smiles.

A father waded with his small children. They had their pants and sleeves rolled. They collected mussels and crabs and the small octopuses that the signs on the beach warned people were protected. Beyond them, old men surfed, their bellies silhouetted against the horizon. They had cracked feet and deep lines around their eyes and walked past us on the beach carrying yellowing longboards.

"These guys have been surfing here since they were kids," said Farouk.

He took off his shoes and dug his feet into the sand without rolling up his cuffs or worrying that they'd drag. And he told me about his family.

He said that his grandmother had taught him how to catch dragonflies with his hands, and his grandfather wore a suit every day. Farouk told me the whole story about how his dad had broken the law and moving to California was the only way he could avoid jail.

His father had put the condo in his mother's name and the rest of the homes and cars were in both names. As part of the settlement the company kept everything his father had owned.

"He stole money, a lot of money," Farouk said. "The company took back what they could, but there was just nothing more for them to take." He picked up a rock, a perfect circle, deep blue like the ocean.

"Most people would be happy with a condo and a Jaguar," I said.

"We had a lot more. I keep thinking of everything, but how much of it was really ours? I kept my stereo and my clothes and a camera he gave me for my last birthday. Which part of it did my father earn? The knobs and the lens?"

"The whole thing is yours because your dad wanted you to have something nice," I said. And I wondered how much of the things I had was mine because my father wanted me to have nice things and how much was there because he wanted me to keep my mouth shut. Were the jeans I was wearing to keep me covered and warm or were they a way to say thank you for protecting him and Ruth?

"We still have so much junk. Our cupboards are full of china sets and pots and pans no one uses. Our linen closets are full of stereos and televisions and phones and sheets for beds we left behind. It makes me crazy."

"Take one thing at a time and bring it to my house. We have nothing. Our walls are bare. We have three sets of sheets and just the towels in our bathrooms," I said, and laughed. It seemed so funny to me while I said it.

"Your dad's a bachelor. What do you expect?"

"My dad isn't a bachelor. I told you, his girlfriend lives with us."

"If he weren't a bachelor, he'd marry her," said Farouk, and brushed the sand from his hands.

"He won't marry her or anyone else. This is as close as he gets."

My dad had told me that a number of times. He'd said, "I'll never find another woman I love enough to marry."

"Why doesn't she buy anything? She should want to have a comfortable home, make her mark." He smiled at me. He stood and offered his hand. He had to get back and open his books, take notes on formulas and equations that he already knew so his father would think he'd been studying all day.

I took his hand and the sand between our hands scraped my palm. He pulled me and I couldn't say why Ruth never bought anything for the house. I never thought that she would or could, but of course it was her home too.

"Maybe she doesn't want to offend my dad," I said.

Farouk held my hand and led me away from the exposed reef and the family with their bags of mussels.

"Maybe she wants to make a fast getaway," he said. We walked up the steep staircase with netting covering the cliff's side so the rocks and gravel wouldn't slide. Water dripped down the side. Swimmers walked below me and showered under the small spigot strapped to one of the beams of the stairs. All the water and the wood seemed like a bad design to me.

"She loves my dad too much," I said. And Ruth had nowhere to go. Her father was dead and her mother lived in Texas. She'd never gone to visit since she'd lived with us, and her mother rarely called. Ruth's friends had gradually stopped calling during the first year.

"Maybe she's a bachelor like he is."

Farouk's heels were rimmed with the white sand from the beach and for a moment I worried that he wouldn't clean it all off and his father would know where he was that afternoon, and Farouk would get into trouble and not be able to spend those afternoons with me. Then I heard what he said. Ruth was a bachelor too.

"Women can't be bachelors," I said.

"Sam, you're not a very good feminist. Women can be whatever they want, right?" he asked, stopping and turning to me. I stopped too, and felt wobbly on that step.

"I meant that the word means a single man, not a woman. She can be whatever she wants," I said, and wanted to keep walking, but I didn't think I could get past him on the stairs. The pressure of my body against the railing might make those rusted bolts pull from the soft, frayed wood and the stairs would wander and fall to the sand on top of the swimmers below.

"All right, I think the word is *bachelorette,*" he said.

"She's pregnant." It was so easy to say. The word was round in the air, the *p* and the *g* and the *a* and *e* creating circles and loops.

Farouk looked down at my stomach. "Congratulations."

"She's about four months along. She's very excited."

"I guess she'd better start buying things for the house," he said, and dropped my hand as he turned and walked up the rest of the stairs.

But he opened the car door for me and as I stepped in he knelt next to me. I fastened my seat belt and looked out the window like we were already driving.

He pulled my hair from under the belt and touched my cheek. His thumb dragged one grain of sand across my skin.

"You are quite wonderful," he said, and kissed me. I hadn't turned in time and so he kissed the edge of my mouth. He turned my face and kissed me again. His skin smelled clean and tan like the sand and the ocean air. I raised my hand to touch his face or his arm, but he pulled back and shut my door.

He drove us home, and at a stoplight he showed me how to hold my hands to catch dragonflies, though I couldn't remember ever being close enough to one to snap my fingers shut and trap it between my palms.

Ruth told my father about the baby in the middle of the night when she thought I would be asleep. I heard their mumbling. My father opened the bedroom door and walked down the stairs. I expected to hear the garage door open, but instead he turned the television on and when I woke in the morning there was a heap of blankets on the couch and he had already left for work.

After that, he was there when I got home from my afternoons with Farouk and if he knew I'd been out with a boy, he didn't say anything. We ate dinner together and he didn't mention the baby, but he did tell funny stories about work, or about me as a baby, and Ruth and I would laugh until our stomachs hurt, because when my father felt good, he was a funny man. I didn't see Ruth alone that whole week.

• • •

Once I ditched practice to be with Chloe. Farouk found me before my final class and took my elbow. We leaned against the cold cinder-block wall.

"Run hard today. Run fast and kick those skinny girls' asses." He kissed my cheek and walked away before I could ask him where he was going that afternoon and why he wouldn't spend it with me.

I spent that class nervous about practice. I hadn't been in two days. Maybe I'd taken too many absences and I'd be in trouble. The teacher talked and my heartbeat felt uneven and thick.

Class ended and I wandered past the gym. I knew that if I had gone in I would have gotten over my nervousness and the coach would have excused me again. She'd be pleased that I again had run well. But I saw Chloe in the parking lot unlocking her mom's car.

I called her name too loudly and she jumped and turned and smiled when she saw me.

"My sweet Sam, running away from running today?" she asked, and hugged me. She seemed smaller.

"We're not suiting up today. The coach wanted to work just with the varsity girls," I said, wishing it were true.

"Well, since you aren't going to be spending the afternoon increasing your life span, come home with me. My mom wants me to run errands. A different sort of running, but it would be good to have you." She unlocked and opened my door like we were on a date.

"Madame," she said.

"Home, James," I said, and she nodded and closed my door. She pulled out and I looked for Farouk's car but he was still parked in the teacher lot, which let him avoid the line of cars Chloe and I sat in. "Where are we off to?"

"Post office, market, and I have to drop something off at the Killgores'," she said, shivering and making a face.

"I guess I'll protect you from the ghosts."

"My hero," she said.

I crossed off the list as Chloe pushed the grocery cart and I was very happy to do these normal things in this very normal part of town where people lived in real houses and had lawns to water. Where moms were doing the shopping right next to us.

We carried the bags into her quiet house. Photos of Chloe and her brother hung from the wall in chronological order, Chloe always smiling.

"Let's get this over with," Chloe called from the kitchen.

"You were such a little cutie," I said as she came out of the kitchen holding a loaf of bread wrapped in tinfoil. I reached to pinch her cheek and she held up the bread in defense.

"Still am. But I'm not the man magnet you seem to be."

"Oh yeah, they're all after me." I tried to grab the bread from her.

"I've heard about you and the new boy."

"I'm sure what you've heard is way better than what's really going on."

"I saw you getting into his car. You looked happy." She bit her lower lip and looked away from me.

"Look at you, the romantic. I thought I warned you about that kind of stuff."

"You did, but I don't think you're taking your own advice," she said.

I pretended to stare at a photograph on the wall. A tiny

girl in a ladybug bikini stood in a kids' pool, her hands reaching for the camera. "You were a cute Miss December," I said.

"You tell me when you think I'm ready for the juicy details."

I was too embarrassed to tell her that he'd only kissed me. That it was I who held him tighter when he came close. I pressed his hand to my hip hoping he would move it up or down, but he would always take his hand away and hold my wrist. We'd kiss and his hand would be soft at first and then he'd begin to squeeze and I wouldn't move because as my skin puckered and pinched beneath his fingers I felt all the things he wanted to do with me and for now that was enough. I couldn't explain that it was almost enough to feel his hand on my arm and listen to his voice as he told me stories.

She sighed. "Let's go over and check out the scene of the crime."

We crossed the cul-de-sac and I began to think twice about going over there.

Henry answered the door.

"Hey, my mom made some food for you guys," Chloe said.

We hesitated as we walked in. I was surprised that Henry was as tall as I was.

I recognized their house as Chloe's with everything flipped around. The walls were a yellowish cream and there were exposed beams in the ceiling. The photos on the walls were not of the family but black-and-white landscapes, and close-ups of blurred flowers.

"Thanks," said Henry, and we followed him into the kitchen.

"My parents aren't home," he said. I was close enough to see his hearing aid poking out from behind his ear, and he smelled like clean laundry.

"Okay, I can just leave a note on it," said Chloe.

"You guys can hang out."

"Sam's got to go home."

"Here, let's have some of the bread," said Henry as he unwrapped the foil. Chloe looked at me while his head was down. She wrinkled her forehead.

"We could use a snack," I said, because I understood what it was like to be alone in a house and wish for nothing more than sounds from another person to distract you from yourself.

He sliced the bread and wrapped each piece in a paper towel and handed it to us.

We sat on the couch and Chloe talked about her mom and the bread and the neighborhood.

I looked around the house for signs of Owen. There was a photo on the entertainment center of the whole family standing on the beach, leis around their necks. They all smiled and no one leaned away from anyone else.

"Which classes are you taking?" Chloe asked.

The house felt warm and I sank into the couch and listened as they talked about teachers and the best way to ace a class. Chloe had told me these same things, but I had never been able to make those tricks work. I finished my bread. "May I use the bathroom?"

"It's upstairs, second door on the left," said Chloe.

My feet echoed on the hardwood stairs and I wanted to make my steps harder and faster like Owen's in the days when he was winning meets and getting straight As in school or like the paramedics' must have sounded on their way up on that last day.

Chloe laughed below me. The first door was Henry's room, where the television was on with a video game on pause. Bright red computer blood bathed the screen. The second door was the bathroom and I stepped in and shut the door. There was a door on either side of the room. And I knew that the closed door led to Owen's room.

I touched the cold knob and turned. The door swung open to a boy's room the mirror image of Henry's, but the television was off and the light dim from half-closed curtains. Dust drifted in the thin beams of sunshine. I'd expected the room to be cold, the hairs on my neck to rise, but it was warm and the air felt soft on my skin. It smelled like the outdoors and camping.

Owen's running shoes lay near the closet and his trophies sat on his dresser. The sheets were falling off the bed and a thin film of black dust covered the sheets and pillow. It was grainy under my touch like the fine sand at Swamis. And I remembered an afternoon changing for practice and one of the skinny girls telling her friend that charcoal would make a person vomit.

I brushed my finger on my jeans. I rubbed hard, so hard my finger burned, and I backed out of that room and shut the bathroom door. I flushed the toilet without using it and ran down the stairs.

"Chloe, I really need to get back. I promised Ruth I'd help her clean if I got home early." I stood near the door.

"Sounds good," she said. Henry followed us out, his head bent. He closed the door behind us.

"I really have to get going," I said.

"I'll give you a lift." She opened her mom's car.

"Freaky, wasn't it?" she said after she had pulled out from the cul-de-sac.

We drove from her neighborhood, where sprinklers twisted water in broad arcs and bright white cars parked in driveways, past the empty school and to my house. I was relieved when we said goodbye and I was alone. I had to admit that Chloe was right, and Farouk was right. I was the one who couldn't see the truth.

chapter nine

And then I missed a meet. I'd forgotten that the meet was at our school. When I didn't see school buses lined up, I thought that maybe I'd confused the date and I left with Farouk. The ocean had warmed suddenly after an Indian summer and we wore shorts and waded into the clear blue water at the Shores.

Farouk told me to shuffle my feet so I wouldn't step on a stingray. I didn't believe that there were stingrays in the water so close to San Diego, but as we walked in farther and the water wet my shorts and made them stick to my legs, I felt a flutter in the sand around my ankles and looked down at my toes. A stingray the size of a dinner plate pulsed and shuddered away from me.

That afternoon we won the meet. The next day my homeroom teacher read the morning announcements, and the names of the girls on my team who placed first, second and third. I blushed and dug deep into my chair. I could have won that race. It would have been my first showing.

But as she went on and read about the upcoming cheerleading tryouts and the half-day for teacher evaluations I knew that there were moments in life that were worth sacrificing for.

After I saw that stingray, Farouk dove into the water in his shorts and T-shirt and swam to me. The water he was pushing from his body swirled around my legs like the stingray and he put his arms around me and surfaced. The curls in his hair captured droplets of water and he pressed his wet body against mine. His skin was cool and my clothes became heavy from his.

"Dive in," he said, and kissed my neck beneath my ear.

"I have my clothes on."

And he pulled me under. My shorts and shirt floated around me as the water stung my eyes and my hair rose from my scalp and shoulders. I was light, weightless. And then Farouk pulled me up. But I could have stayed under, watching the sand hover just above the surface, turning blue as a set came in and the water deepened above me while the sun moved farther away.

And so I wasn't nervous when I went to the coach's office to find out what my punishment was. I stood in her doorway, my breathing deep and clear the way she told us to breathe when we lay on the grass picturing our wins.

As I waited for her to look up from the paperwork, I was aware that my body was glowing on the inside through the places Farouk had touched—my hip, the back of my neck and the inside of my thigh that last afternoon after he handed me a towel and I dried myself and my clothes, and despite the surfer boys changing into their wetsuits near us, towels wrapped around their bare bodies, Farouk pressed me against the car door and let himself go too far. With his thumb inside my shorts, he kissed me and tasted like salt and the sea and the moment I sank underwater.

"Sit. We won yesterday," she said.

"Congratulations," I said.

"You would have placed. Your last time was better than third place."

I nodded, but I didn't believe her. The girl who won third was usually one of the fastest girls on the team.

She waited for me to say something, to come up with another excuse for my absence, but I was done with that. I didn't want to lie about where I went in the afternoon. I wasn't a runner. I wasn't a girl who drove herself with the taste of winning. I was a normal girl, a teenager, with a boy whose ears she wanted to bite and whose breath she wanted to hear in her ear as he lay on top of her.

"I should have put you on probation weeks ago, but I thought you would pass through whatever was going on. And I have to take you off the team, but because you didn't get a warning, consider this your warning."

A flush was moving up her neck. This was hard on her. At one time I had listened to her. I believed her when she told me that we could all win and that I was a strong runner with potential. And now I sat in her office and felt nothing.

I wasn't relieved that I was still on the team, that I had another chance, and I wasn't annoyed that she hadn't just cut me off altogether. And because I felt nothing, she knew I didn't believe her any longer.

"I understand," I said. "But I don't think I'll win a meet, and I run faster when I practice on my own, so I don't think I'll come back."

Her face was red and her blue eyes were bright. Her shoulders shivered and she looked at the papers on her desk. She breathed deeply and I counted in my head as she held her breath for ten seconds like she'd told us to do.

"Fine," she said when she was done.

I stepped out of her office and through the locker room. I took my lock off the locker and pressed my shoes and shorts into my backpack. The girls around me didn't look up as I left. They were talking to each other or stretching with their legs on the benches.

I opened the door of the locker room. The sun was so bright my eyes ached and the walls and the sidewalk all blended together white and yellow and hot. I walked, letting my eyes adjust. I stood at the edge of the parking lot and saw Farouk's white car, in the middle of the lot. As I walked toward him through the waves floating from the pavement, my heart felt weightless, rising from my body.

One afternoon I came home early. We'd been on the beach climbing over rocks and stepping in tidal pools. Our aim was to get to the nude beach, Black's Beach, where men picked each other up and the pros braved the hike down the cliff to surf the big waves.

We could see the surfers in the distance, small black dots hovering above the ocean, and we were walking toward them when the clouds moved overhead. They were heavy, gray clouds and the air became wet. I saw a single flash in the sky and heard the rain on the water like a wave constantly breaking.

"I think we should go," said Farouk. I stood for a moment, confused, trying to remember the last thunderstorm I'd seen during the day. It seemed like storms happened at night and ended by the morning so that all that remained were puddles and gray spots on car hoods. San Diego was a desert backed up to the ocean. When rain was coming people talked about it for days before the storm. We picked our way back over the rocks beneath the cliff.

"I've never seen this happen before," I said. I wanted to watch, to feel the rain on my skin with my feet in the ocean, digging my toes into the soft sand.

"Sam, I know science isn't your strong suit, but you really don't want to be around water during a lightning storm." He took my hand to pull me back from the ocean. The clouds had covered the sun and it was dark like night was falling.

"The surfers aren't leaving," I said, watching them in the water.

"I don't think taking cues from surfers is in our best interest."

My legs became cold, and a single arm of lightning struck the water near the horizon.

My heel skidded over moss clinging to the rock and Farouk caught my elbow before I fell. The ocean had turned gray and the tide had come up over some of the rocks we'd walked on earlier. The rain hit us as we leapt off the final rock into the sand. We ran to the car, the heavy sand clinging to my shoes. I felt like I did when I ran in nightmares, my legs pumping, my muscles burning but never moving as fast as I needed to.

Our clothes were soaked when we reached the car. My hair pulled my scalp and dripped onto my shorts. Farouk reached into the glove compartment and handed me a clump of paper napkins.

"Too late for that," I said.

He turned on the heater and opened the vents, moving his hand in front of each one to make sure the heat was blowing toward me. Drops the size of nickels pounded the windshield, and blurry figures ran to their cars, towels over their heads.

We still had two hours to be together before he'd have to leave.

"Take me home so I can change and you can dry off," I said.

He took a piece of my hair that had fallen out of my ponytail and pressed it between his fingers. A single drop fell into his palm.

"Okay," he said.

He drove slowly, following the hazy taillights ahead of us. The rain eased, so he drove faster and he made a turn too quickly. I felt the back tires give way just for a second before he got the car under control and drove on like it hadn't happened.

It was sprinkling at my house. The usual silence greeted me as I opened the door.

"This is my family's vacation villa," I said as we stepped

into the family room we never used. Cream leather couches surrounded a sharp glass coffee table and though the housecleaner came once a week, I don't think she dusted the couches. The room was dim, gray light peeking through the blinds.

"You can see that if you brought over some of your things, we'd be even," I said. And we walked up the stairs to the kitchen and dining area.

"This is where our chef cooks my meals," I said as we came up the stairs, and as I turned I saw Ruth sitting at the table.

I jumped and she smiled at me. Farouk pushed up the stairs behind me.

"This is the chef," I said. And Ruth stood. She wore a tight shirt and pants I didn't recognize and her stomach was round and solid beneath her clothes. I hadn't realized she was showing.

"This is the boy who drives the Jaguar," I said. And Farouk moved from behind me toward Ruth.

She shook his hand and he said his name again like he'd said it that first day, the last syllable like a kiss in my ear. I hadn't said his name the right way since we met. It came out of my mouth long and awkward.

"Out playing in the rain?" she asked.

"Cross-country was canceled," I said loudly, and Farouk turned and looked at me. "We went to the beach," I said. And both were watching me. My excuses became confused in my mind: If cross-country had been canceled because of the weather, why would we go to the beach? When Farouk saw me struggling he turned back to Ruth.

"We left when we saw the lightning," he said.

"There are some towels in the bathroom, dry off," she said. "I'll make tea."

Farouk went into the bathroom and I went to my room and changed from my wet clothes into jeans and a sweater and tried to fix my hair, to push back the small hairs pulled from my ponytail, curling and floating around my face. But they wouldn't go back in. I took the rubber band out and my hair was just wet enough that the ends caught and snapped and long strands fell to the floor. If I brushed it without conditioner, the knots would cause more hair to break. So I walked back downstairs with my hair wild, drying in black tangles down my back.

Farouk held a photo. "I'm going to be a doctor. My family's full of them."

"You could be a pediatrician and care for this little one. Check out the baby picture," she said to me as I sat down with them.

Farouk handed the photo to me. I was expecting an infant posed among pillows and stuffed animals, but it was a blurry, gray picture with swirls like the water in the tidal pools at the beach.

"I was at the doctor's this afternoon and I had my first sonogram," she said. "That's the baby."

She stood and poured water into the mugs. I pulled the photo away from my face and brought it close again, and I traced the darker areas with my thumb.

"I can't see it," I said.

"Me neither," she said, and laughed. She shrugged. "He told me what we were looking at but I just nodded and smiled."

"Are you sure this isn't one of those ink tests? Maybe

instead of a baby, you're supposed to say butterfly, or banana," I said.

"I say Jacuzzi," she said, and brought our mugs. The tea was hot on my tongue.

"I say my eyelids after I rub my eyes," I said.

"Give it to the doctor; he'll explain it to us," she said, and I handed the photo back to Farouk.

Farouk took the photo and looked at me and Ruth, raised his eyebrow and turned the photo around the right way. He held it next to his shoulder like a teacher who was reading a picture book to children and he cleared his throat.

"The baby is in a good position, head pointed down." He tapped at a white bubble.

"The amniotic fluid is at a healthy level; hands and feet are forming." He drew circles with his finger around the center, around the tidal pools and black oil spills. He turned the picture back to him and looked closely, then turned it around again.

"The interesting thing is the cell formation. I can tell by the way the baby sits that it will be a redhead like its mother."

He pressed the photo on the table and rested his fingertips in the pools and closed his eyes.

"And from the sound waves still floating from the paper, I can tell he will be pretty, and crazy just like his sister."

Ruth laughed before I got the joke. Until she laughed, his *crazy* burned inside me.

"What kind of doctor are you?" she said, and snatched the sonogram away. She turned it the way she'd had it before and smoothed it down. She smiled at him and rolled her eyes at me.

Farouk stuck out his hand and held it straight, palm down over the table.

"I'm going to be a surgeon. Nerves of steel," he said. His hand was still without his having to breathe deeply or look away. Ruth and I put out our hands. Ruth's skin looked soft, freshly washed. And my hand was small next to theirs, my nails short and cut in strange angles by the clippers I took from my father's medicine cabinet. My hand did not shake, but my thumb strayed to the side, and only with the deepest concentration could I make it still.

"I could be a surgeon too," I said. Both of them turned to look at me. My hand began to shake and no amount of breathing or focus could calm it down.

Farouk left after seeing my room, but before my father came home. I wanted them to meet, but I didn't protest when he said he had to leave, or say that my dad would be home in just thirty minutes. My dad had called, stuck in traffic, and I knew he would be home. Instead, I said that Farouk would have to see my room before he left. And so Ruth turned her back and washed the mugs for much longer than it normally would have taken her, but she wanted to tell us she wasn't worried about the things we might do up there. And I didn't want to do those things then, in my room. I wanted to go someplace lovely for that, someplace with the sun on Farouk's skin so I could look up and see him glowing orange and gold.

We stood in the doorway of my room and once we were there I was unsure why I'd brought him up there. It was a room, a bed against one wall, clothes in a closet and more stuffed into drawers, a desk and a chair. And like the rest of the house my room had no photos on the walls and no pictures in frames sitting on the bookshelves. But he would know it was my room because of the blank walls, and he wouldn't get it confused with other girls' rooms that held posters of bands and photos of family vacations, and dried corsages hanging from a tack in the wall.

He moved into the room and looked up at the vaulted ceiling, where I noticed cobwebs deep in the corners far higher than the housekeeper's broom. I took his arm and showed him the bathroom; I didn't want him looking at the dirty places no one could reach. He turned on the movie star lights around my vanity and pulled his cheeks in and fluffed imaginary hair in the mirror.

"I obviously use those quite a bit," I said.

He did not look at my bed or sit on it and bounce. Instead, he acted like it wasn't there. He never once looked down or over at the sheets that were still crumpled on one side from my body that morning and the dreams I'd had in the night, while the other side was straight and empty.

He looked through my sliding glass door and into the college boy's room and for a moment I was afraid that the boy would see Farouk in my room and know that I was a girl who had boys up to her room. A girl who dreamt of leaning against a rock on the beach, Farouk holding me against that rock with the pressure from his body.

But no one was home and Farouk turned away from the window.

"This is a princess's room."

I was standing close to him, close enough to lean over and kiss his neck.

"I could climb up the balcony to you. Rescue you from all of this," he said.

"Rescue me from what?" I asked.

"I'll show you places where the sun rises over the ocean and sets behind mountains," he said. He pulled his hand through my hair. It tugged and stung my scalp.

I listened to Ruth beneath us putting away our mugs and running the water. If I unbuttoned my shirt and then unbuttoned his, and if I pressed his hand into my underwear just a bit too roughly, she would not hear if Farouk let go and did what he wanted and I wanted. We would be very quiet, quiet like I'd been in the front seat of a truck, with a boy I met on the same beach I'd been at today. The truck's windows were cracked, people passing through the parking lot just a few car lengths away.

He moved away from me and touched my books, novels for high school and thin books from when I was a kid. After I moved into this condo, I woke one morning and found boxes and boxes outside the front door softening and leaning from the dewy morning. I pulled them in and found them full of things from my childhood that I had forgotten about but my mother had kept. She'd given them back to me, though I had no idea what to do with them. My dad and I went through them and got rid of the dolls and toys and stained dresses, but I kept my books.

But with Farouk's thick finger over them, I was embarrassed that I had kept them.

"Why is it so cold in here?" he asked.

"The sun hits in the morning," I said, though the sun rarely hit my room, except in the middle of August. After

Farouk said it, I noticed how when he was not near me my fingers grew stiff.

I went to him and kissed the back of his neck, the little mole just beneath his hairline pressing into my lip. He turned and kissed me once on the mouth, and I held the hem of his heavy, cold shirt, ready to pull it over his head. But again he moved away from me.

"I want to shower, get changed," he said, and so I let him go. He walked out ahead of me and I shut my door behind me to keep in his smell, and his warmth. As I turned, I remembered when I was a kid and a girl told me that if I stood in a small room with the lights off and if I breathed once, twice and then ran for the door and shut it quick enough behind me, my soul would stay inside that room waiting for me to open the door and take it back. I hoped that when I opened the door part of Farouk would be waiting and ready for me as I came back in.

chapter ten

We were released for two weeks for Christmas as the air grew dry and smelled thick and dusty like a heater left on too long. People at the mall would look out at the clear sky, the air still warm enough to wear short sleeves, and shake their heads, thinking of the snowplows in the East that we saw on the news. I looked forward to sleeping in and spending quiet mornings in my house, alone. Chloe promised we would have breakfast at a diner at the beach. "We'll eat huevos rancheros and tons of hash browns."

And I looked forward to afternoons with Farouk.

But these afternoons were shorter. There was less sun, less time to be outside. Night fell over us before we could reach Swamis and return. So we stayed closer to home and he'd spend a few minutes at my house. Ruth was working later. He'd come in and sit at the table, and I'd sit next to him and kiss his neck and mouth with the glass tabletop in my side. And he would kiss me back. Close to the time he knew he had to go home, he would let me sit on his lap, my legs around his hips, his hands on my thighs pressing and tilting me in small circles up and over him.

A few days before Christmas, Farouk left as Ruth was pulling around the corner. I saw them wave as she passed and I blushed for the things she must have thought we were doing. She honked her horn as she turned off the engine and I came down the stairs expecting groceries. She opened the trunk. Inside were dusty boxes with yellowed plastic windows showing Christmas ornaments.

"I dug them out of my storage space," she said. I'd had no idea she had a storage space. I'd thought all of her things were in our house. And I remembered what Farouk had said. Did she have a whole life in there boxed and ready to be moved into a real life in a proper home?

"We don't have a tree," I said.

I hadn't had a tree since I was a kid and only once was it a real tree we picked out at a lot. It was after my father left and I still lived with my mother. She had said, "I'm sick of the fake tree. It's bent and sickly. We'll go get a real one. I saw a lot on the way home from work."

It was nighttime and I had already bathed, but my mother took me out with a sweatshirt over my pajamas. I was excited to be out in the dark. My mom lifted her eyebrows at me and smiled. "We're breaking all the rules."

We went to the tree lot and chose a small tree that would

fit on top of the car. The guy at the tree lot offered to lift it to the roof.

"If I can't lift it onto the roof, how will I get it inside?" she said, and took the tree from him. She lifted the tree in one fluid sweep. We decorated it with a few ornaments and some ribbons she had found in the back of a drawer. She lit it for the first few nights, but soon I was the one lighting the tree and sitting near it. It grew dry before Christmas came.

"I'm going to throw it out," she said.

"Okay," I said. But she didn't. And she lit it on Christmas morning for me when I woke.

Ruth and I drove east to a run-down mall where trees had been propped up on the hot tar of the parking lot. Ruth wore white linen and a straw hat to keep the sun from her face. Her stomach showed and she smiled at me with small bits of sun sprinkled over her face. She looked like she was on vacation on some far-off European island.

She ran her hands through the thick trees and the smell of pine surrounded us. I knew she was doing this so that I would know it was Christmas, so that it would be real and happy for me.

We chose a tree with a dent in one side, but the rest was full and green and small enough to fit on the top of Ruth's car. We brought it into the house and faced the dented side into the corner of the living room.

We hung the balls and tried our best to dust them and if we did rub off some of the color, we turned those parts away. When we were finished, we stood back and took in the whole room. The tree leaned just a little, and the ornaments looked old but as if they were part of an important tradition. We lit a fire in the fireplace, which had been cold since we moved in, and the colors in the room changed from cool grays and white to orange and gold; it was warm, a family room, a living room.

We waited for my dad to get home. We sat at the table, barely getting up, as if our moving might make him miss the tree altogether. Ruth made dinner late. We'd finished eating and had washed the plates and put them away when he came home.

The tree was in a corner he couldn't see as he passed the family room. He didn't smell the green smell that had traveled through the house or see the blue and green and red glow from the lights.

He nearly missed us, standing still in the kitchen waiting for him.

"What are you guys doing in the dark? Let's shed a little light on the subject," he said, and the kitchen light popped and buzzed.

"We were going to surprise you," said Ruth.

"What else could you two surprise me with?"

Ruth led him by the arm down the stairs to the tree. We stood for a moment. He nodded. He ran his palm over the needles and held a small star Ruth had made from aluminum foil and pipe cleaners when she was a child.

"Looks good," he said, and dropped the star. He turned to walk back up the stairs to pick at the leftovers.

"It's Christmas," said Ruth, "and we're a family now."

"Nothing says family like a Christmas tree." He pulled the knot from his tie.

"We got this for you," she said. Her voice was loud and her words echoed.

"It's very like you to give me something I didn't ask for,"

he said with a smile, his eyebrows raised. It was a light tone, but the last step before he became mad.

Her feet were flat on the floor, fists at her sides. She was ready for the fight. How much would her baby hear?

"I'll vacuum and water and make sure nothing stains the carpet," I said, stepping between them.

"We did this so you would be happy, and we would be happy, and for just a few days your daughter would know what the rest of the world does for Christmas," she said.

"You did this for you," he said. "Christmas trees mean nothing to me or to her."

And I knew this was true, because while the tree was lovely and smelled nice, it didn't trigger memories or a joy that I imagined in others. But I was ready to tell Ruth about how my life was complete now. That it was all I had ever wanted from my father.

"Just take a moment to pretend to be grateful," she said, quiet again.

He turned and walked up the stairs. Ruth followed, but stopped in the kitchen. She turned off the lights and when we heard the shower upstairs she went up to their room. I sat on the sofa and watched the tree, waiting for the first snowfall or the reindeers' hooves on the roof. Waiting for some sign that this was a meaningful time of year, a change.

It was quiet in their room when I went up to bed. My father had left the space heater on for me like he always did and I knew that this meant he wasn't mad at me and he expected me to act like nothing happened, which I would because he had taught me well.

I lay in my bed. My room was orange from the heater, and a breeze came from the sliding glass door, which I had left open just a crack. I heard the first tap on the glass as I was drifting off and I thought that it was the window hot on the inside and cool on the outside, expanding or contracting. There was another tap. Another. I got out of bed to shut the door. And then the taps came like rain and I heard a whisper. I opened the door and stepped outside, my feet cold on the wood balcony.

Farouk was below me, smiling.

"I'll climb up," he said.

"You could have called," I said as he pulled himself up from the patio below me, which I hadn't used since we moved here. His hands were at my feet between the slats of the balcony.

"This is more fun," he said.

I backed away from the edge because I could feel his weight pulling the balcony down. He swung his legs over the railing and smiled at me, out of breath.

"What did you think of that?" he said, and brushed his hands on his thighs. He wore shorts and a sweatshirt.

"I'm flattered," I said, "but I don't get it."

"Nothing to get." He kissed my cheek as he opened the door wider and let himself into my room. We were whispering, but with each breath I felt like we were shouting, like at any moment my dad would find this boy in my room who had climbed up my balcony.

"Put some clothes on," he said, and turned off my heater. "We're going out."

I pulled on jeans, and a top still warm from my body. Farouk opened the sliding door again for me. I looked over the edge and it seemed much higher with him behind me than with him below.

"We can just go out the front door. My dad would never hear," I said. The air was moist and salty from the ocean.

"I'll go first," he said. I watched where he placed his feet, what he held on to before he lowered himself onto the patio below. I stepped as he did. My hands were sweating and splinters pinched my skin as I lowered myself.

He caught me as I jumped down, and I was sweating cold, and he was hot, dry in the wet night air.

"You're very brave," he said, and took my hand. As we walked to the car a light at the college boy's house turned on and his blinds parted and I held my breath. Maybe he had watched us in the dark.

I leaned as Farouk drove, anticipating turns that didn't come, and I didn't ask where we were going because there was quiet all around us. The radio was off and the streets were empty. Streetlights blinked red like we were in a small town with not enough traffic to keep the lights on. We drove into a condo complex like my own and into the maze of tan buildings. He parked in the driveway of one I would never be able to find again.

I followed him through a small gate and I looked for something that would help me remember this house, but the patio was empty, like the others that surrounded it.

"No parents? No dad to make sure you're doing your homework?" I asked.

"No, they're out of town for the night. Conference in Los Angeles. They'll be back tomorrow sometime."

He opened the front door and as I stepped inside I recognized his smell. The air was warm and a night-light was on in another room, showing walls covered with paintings. The carpet was thick and lumpy.

There was too much furniture, bulky leather sofas and pale brocade chairs and dark, heavy tables with wrought-iron legs. The room was dense with spicy air. Farouk didn't turn on a light and I was worried about stubbing a toe or banging my shin into the unseen edge of a table.

He put his keys on a dining room table that sat in a breakfast nook connected to the living room. The table held piles of papers and empty glasses and its legs ended in claws clutching balls. It was probably an antique.

"My parents couldn't get rid of everything," he said. "Somehow they made it all fit here."

He stepped around things easily, used to the small path that wound around the room and into the kitchen. But I nearly tripped. I knelt down. The carpet was rugs and rugs piled on top of each other. In the hazy light, I could see that the one I stood on was navy blue or nearly black with leaves and flowers growing from the borders. Two other rugs were beneath. One stretched out to the dining table and bunched below a window and one appeared in patches under other rugs layered on top of it.

I ran my palm over the carpets. All were dense and warm under my touch. I dug my fingers into the pile and could barely feel the bottom.

"Careful," he said. "Those are our family heirlooms."

I pulled my fingers out like I had been shocked.

"Kidding, they've been around for generations. If they

can't handle a girl's fingers in them, then they're crap," he said, and knelt down in front of me.

He backed up and motioned for me to get close and in the dim light he put his hand on the carpet beneath him.

"What does it look like?" he said. My eyes were growing used to the light and I could make out a path between green squares. Trees grew in the squares and small red birds flew over the paths.

"It's a garden," I said.

"It's a map," he said, and backed away so I could see the whole thing. And I looked hard for the map, for the line that would lead someone where they needed to go. It wasn't until he showed me the birds that I figured it out. They pointed at each other, each beak facing the next bird through those small plots of green with their trees and flowers and vines until the end where a small group of birds gathered in the final square.

"You must spend a lot of time on the floor." I would never have thought to look that close. I wouldn't have thought that a carpet could be more than something that kept my steps quiet in the night, or my feet warm.

"When I was a kid my mom showed me. She made up stories for the birds in that last tree. Sometimes they were having my birthday party and sometimes they were scared of a wolf or a dragon or a cat."

He rubbed his hand over the garden slowly, then fast as if trying to erase it.

"There are more," he said, and stood. And I stood and looked again at the garden, but it was just squares under my feet, the birds small spots.

He opened a heavy cabinet that held a television with a stereo and CDs wedged in. It seemed strange that Farouk's family had things so modern behind the doors of something so old.

He pressed a CD into the stereo and the music was the music of carnivals and carousels. A woman sang in a language I was pretty sure was French and though the music felt happy, her voice was impossibly sad.

"Edith Piaf," he said. "Have you heard of her?"

"I feel like we should be doing the cancan." I grabbed an invisible skirt around my waist and shook my hips to the music.

"It makes me want to drink coffee and think important thoughts." He put a finger on his chin.

"You don't seem to need music for that," I said. As I listened to that woman sing and watched Farouk pose for me, he seemed so much older, and I so much younger. I was just a silly California girl whose only culture was the books teachers forced her to read in school and Beach Boys concerts that followed Padres baseball games. I had nothing to offer this boy, who had seen the world and knew about singers who sang in different languages, in far-off places and far-off times.

He sat again on the floor where two rugs met, their fringes tangled together. He pulled me to him and I sat in the knot of his legs.

"This one's my favorite," he said, and leaned into me, pointing with his arms around me.

"It's a portrait rug," he said, "my father's pride and joy."

It traveled under the coffee table, which was heavy with books and cluttered with empty cups and opened envelopes. I lay on my side to see the whole thing and with Farouk behind me warming my back and that woman singing about what I was sure were tragedies, I knew why it was his favorite.

A woman with long black hair and eyes like Farouk's poured water from a jug. She sat above a man and looked down on him. Her water was pale and flowed in a stream to the man, who held a goblet to catch it. They were outside with more water behind them and bushes hiding them from others. She smiled at him and poured. It wasn't a portrait for a family to hang on their wall and remember their ancestors; it was for these two to remember a moment when giving him water was enough, and when he was still there to catch it.

"I understand," I said, though he hadn't asked.

"Good," he said, and he lay down next to me. He put his hand on my arm as I traced that water in the goblet and as I ran my finger through her hair, which was as long as the water.

And I let him kiss my neck and my shoulder and my stomach as he took my shirt off without kissing my mouth. And I didn't take my finger from that rug until we were both naked and he was over me, his warm skin glowing gold and brown in the faint light.

This was all I had ever wanted, this beautiful boy filling me, his breath on my neck making me warm, and hot and cold. My heart beat in my ears as he leaned in close and then it was his heart I heard. He lay on top of me and I couldn't breathe, but I knew that my heart would keep beating and as he raised his hips I took small breaths.

And with Farouk inside me, I thought of Owen. I thought of Owen because I was sure that as his heart had swelled and stopped, he had felt the same freedom I did with those French words pouring over us and Farouk whispering my name. Samantha, the way I knew it should be pronounced.

Farouk tensed, and relaxed, and it was over. He kissed my eyes and my mouth and left me. And I lay listening to the music, his warmth leaving my skin slowly. I lay there until he returned, my legs closed, my hand over my belly.

He came back with shorts on and no shirt, his hair wet like it had been in the hot, dry fall days when we spent afternoons in the warm water. He brought me a robe that I knew was his from the smell as he draped it around my shoulders. He pointed the bathroom out to me and I went in and waited before I cleaned myself. I waited until I had told my body that things were right. I tried to count from my last period, but I had never kept track of it before—boys in the past had used protection. I tried to think that that night was a good night. One of only a few nights of the month that the sex ed teacher had told us we could become pregnant. I believed it as much as I could, hoping to change my body's chemistry or at least reassure it that this was okay.

I breathed deeply and thought of my mother. She'd told me that when she was pregnant with me, she knew she would keep the baby.

"There had been one before, but we'd lost it. 'I'm keeping this one,' I told myself," she'd said. "I told myself, 'I'm keeping it. Body, there's nothing you can do about it.' And that's how we got you."

I wanted to believe like my mother had. I wanted that determination to order my body around. This was right, I told myself. I yelled it in my head. This was a boy I loved, and he loved me and we would be very happy together thinking important thoughts and doing the cancan late into the night.

• • •

The rest of the house was just as he had described it—cluttered and full of things they would never use or need again. A closet upstairs held kitchen appliances; sheets and towels sat in a corner near the stairs. His parents' bed was unmade and sitting on the floor without a frame.

What he didn't tell me about was the mess I would find, and the thin layer of dust and hair covering the carpets so that we left footprints, and the shreds of paper scattered like a trail through the hallway. The bathroom walls were spotted with black mold and the kitchen counters were covered with days-old plates of food, pots holding dried and yellowed rice, teacups with rings of brown and a small puddle in the bottom. But there was no smell in the house beyond Farouk, warm and brown and full of spices.

The mess stopped in his room. His closet held only his own clothes and there were no rugs, just the pale carpet that probably covered the whole house. His bed sat against the wall beneath a window that looked out to the street below, his car's trunk just barely in view. The covers were crisp and neatly folded under a pillow. Posters of waves breaking on an empty beach and snow blowing over a mountain peak were hung on the walls perfectly spaced, their tops straight lines against the white walls. And one black-and-white photo sat framed on his dresser. It was a man with the same skin as Farouk wearing sunglasses and a suit, stepping off a plane. The man smiled with his mouth closed and one eyebrow raised. He was very handsome and reminded me of an old movie star.

"It's my grandfather," Farouk said.

"He's very suave," I said. "Very handsome."

"He's coming from Iran to California soon. He'll be here

for a few months. I haven't seen him in years." Farouk touched the photo and the frame moved just a hair but I knew it was straighter now, and that he'd been able to tell as soon as we walked in the room that the photo was crooked.

"I can't go to Iran. They'll recruit me into the army. And then my family would have to pay them to get me out," he said.

I looked closer at the picture, at the background, to see what Iran looked like. I would have guessed desert and women with heavy veils over their faces and men with dusty sandals on their feet. But I saw an airport like any other. A long strip of asphalt and other, larger planes in the background. No clues except this man in a suit and sunglasses like the ones Farouk wore on the days we drove to the beach right into that glowing orange sunset.

I looked down at his bed and considered sitting and then bouncing and then curling up and wrapping myself in the blankets that I was sure held his smell. But I wouldn't unless he did because I knew I didn't belong here. This was a boy's room, his space, and I remembered Owen's room and the dust and the mess and the secrets it held—secrets I should never have found. I wanted to back out of the room carefully before the bad parts of Farouk were revealed.

"I've never seen snow," I said, hoping that would be enough. I hoped he would turn away from that poster and ask me about myself and lead me away and make plans to take me to the tall mountains the people from my school visited on weekends. And I hoped that my stepping back from the bed would make him realize that I knew I was in danger of seeing too much of him.

"Never?" he said.

"Never," I said. "The closest I've seen is when I was a kid

and we went to Sea World. They had a machine set up that blew snow in an arc over mounds and kids were sledding down them."

"You could fill a book with the things you haven't seen." He kissed my cheek and I laughed. I laughed because what I didn't tell him would have made me seem even more pathetic. I couldn't tell him that the day I saw the snow was in the middle of summer.

"Books are already filled with them," I said, "and posters and television shows."

"You'll see them one day." He hugged me and then pulled back. I had to look away as he looked at my face. His breath was on my cheek and I held so still my arms quivered. I tried to leave my face blank so my own secrets would not be revealed, but I wanted to cry while he looked at me so closely.

"I don't believe what they say about you," he said.

And I let go of the breath that I hadn't realized I had been holding. When I did, I grew dizzy and for a second I thought I'd pass out. He pulled away and my arms stopped shaking and I straightened up. Because there it was—the secret I had been holding on to. I had told him the other secrets. I'd told him about my father and he had seen Ruth. He'd seen my room, empty like no one in particular lived there. And there was the final secret revealed not by me but by the school, by the boys and the girls who suspected but never truly knew.

When Chloe and I left that smudgy spot below the bridge I had known that someone would find it. I'd hoped it would be someone who believed that I was a girl who didn't sleep with boys she didn't know. But I understood that people would believe a dead high school sports star over an invisible girl.

"If you don't believe it, then why did you tell me?" I

wanted to stay right there in his room and hunt until I discovered his last secret. Maybe the reason they moved would turn out to be more shameful than stealing money or so boring he'd had to make up something to impress the first girl he met.

"You seemed like it was your first time tonight."

I turned from him and looked at his closet. I could pretend I was cold and needed a jacket.

"It wasn't," I said. The words were light and left me in a breeze. And after I heard them in the room I too felt light. I felt like if I told all the secrets I would float away.

"Me either," he said. I watched him closely, but not as closely as he had watched me, because he told me everything I needed to know.

He crossed his arms and then uncrossed them and told me about a girl in the woods behind his house. He said he'd known her from school and that they agreed to meet one afternoon in the trees. He brought a blanket and as they began, it started snowing. Just a light dusting, enough to make her damp, though they weren't cold.

"She had hair like yours," he said, and he pulled just a few strands like he had at the beach.

"She was very lucky," I said because in that moment I knew that I was the lucky one. I was the real first girl.

"I was very lucky," he said, and pulled me close to him and kissed me on the forehead and on the cheek and on the mouth. And I was back on solid ground. I wished I could take my secret back because after that night I wouldn't be sure what he believed. Whether he believed that it was my first time and I had lied like he had, or whether he believed what the others had told him and what I had admitted.

• • •

He dropped me off at home and I didn't even think of climbing back up my balcony. That part of the night was so far away. I knew that I could simply walk through the front door and return to my bed as if time had not moved forward since he'd thrown pebbles at my window.

The sky was a dark gray and my eyelashes felt wet from the ocean air that had traveled so far inland.

I put my key in the door and unlocked it slowly, listening for the two clicks. I turned back to Farouk. He kissed my mouth and then each cheek.

"You are very beautiful in the night," he said. And I kissed him back so he wouldn't see me blush.

"Thank you for showing me your house," I said when the heat in my face had passed.

"Goodbye, Sam," he said, and turned away from me and walked back to his car. And I could barely breathe. That goodbye sounded like he would never see me again. I waited for him to drive away and I stood still for a few minutes more listening in the muffled silence. And when I didn't hear anything I stepped inside, walked up the stairs and got back into my bed as if I'd been sleeping all night.

If it hadn't been so late, I would have called my mother. I would have told her there was a boy I loved. A boy who finally loved me. "You're very lucky," she would have said, "but he's even luckier." But even if I had heard her say that I would know it couldn't be true.

• • •

Farouk called on Christmas Eve. When the phone rang, I was in bed reading, though it wasn't late.

"Hey, kiddo," he said. My face grew cold and hot all at once.

"Hey, stranger," I said. "Why aren't you in bed waiting for Santa?"

"We're going to a party tonight. Family thing. My parents feel like we need to connect with the other Persian families in San Diego."

"Sounds like a good chance for them to make some friends," I said. I was disappointed because that meant he wouldn't surprise me late in the night with pebbles thrown against my window.

"All the Persians are crazy."

"All but you," I said.

"No, the men are okay; it's the women you have to look out for."

"Well, stay close to the guys tonight."

"Don't worry," he said. "Listen, my dad was pretty pissed that I haven't done much studying lately. I just wanted to tell you in case I couldn't call for a while."

And while he told me about how his father had yelled at him, I smiled just a bit. I smiled because Farouk had taken a risk for me. He thought being with me was more important than work. But what I didn't think was why he didn't do the work when I wan't there. He could have done it easily in the evenings.

"Okay," I said. "I guess I want you to be smart and to get into medical school."

"You're so generous. I have to go. My dad has the car started."

"Have fun," I said.

"I always do," he said, and hung up.

I wasn't worried about what I had told him. Not all the time. But some nights I woke in the middle of the night, breathless, perfectly awake. I must have been dreaming about the moment when I told him that I was the girl he'd heard about because when I woke it was as if I was back in that room with the choice to make again. And in my own room in the darkness and the cold because the heater had long ago shut itself off, I tested myself to make sure I would say the same thing again. And I thought that I would because I was that girl. I was a girl some boys would call a slut.

But I wasn't that girl too and maybe I should have thought for a moment more before telling him. I could have told him that I had been that girl in the past but that I had changed since him. I was a new girl with new thoughts and new places I'd been and stories I'd heard. I was a girl who knew there was a world out there just for me. I could have said, "No."

These thoughts would come back as I slept so I wasn't sure until the morning whether I had gone back and told him something different. In the morning I chose to forget it all and feel light and free because a boy thought I was worth climbing up a balcony for. A smart boy who understood chemical reactions, and symbolism in literature and numbers. He understood the value of things.

Just before New Year's my mom drove down from Berkeley. "It has to be a late Christmas," she'd said on the phone. "I can't get any other time off work."

Chloe picked me up, excited to see my mom. "Do you think she'll bring you cool San Francisco things?" she said on our way to breakfast.

"Like what? A jigsaw puzzle of Alcatraz?" I was nervous, because there was a lot to tell my mom, and more not to tell her.

"No, just something cool from Haight Street. Like a CD from a band we've never heard of."

"I don't see my mom music shopping."

"I bet she has something good."

We met her at a café near the beach. She sat reading a book, with tea for the three of us already poured and steaming in our mugs.

"Miss Chloe," she said, and they hugged.

"Miss Samantha," said my mom, and she looked me over once, tucked some hair behind my ear and hugged me, too.

She wore a pale brown sweater with bell sleeves, and faded blue jeans. Her hair, like mine, was thick and pulled back in a heavy silver clip.

"Loving the Berkeley you," said Chloe as we sat.

"Chloe, my dear, *I'm* loving the Berkeley me."

"Is it just totally great? Are you marching and singing and protesting and reading great books?" Chloe asked.

I put my teacup down too hard and hot water splashed over my hand. "Chloe, this isn't the Summer of Love. My mother works at a lamp shop. She lives in Oakland."

"North Oakland. Very close to Berkeley, Sam." My mom closed her menu and rested her chin in her palms. She smiled at me and winked at Chloe.

"I'm not protesting, but I am reading great books. When

you come up, you can march and have sit-ins and I'll bail you out of jail."

"Perfect," said Chloe. She ran her finger down the list of egg plates.

"What's going on in the land of endless sunshine?"

"Our little Sam has a boy she loves," said Chloe. She raised her eyebrows as she pretended to be very impressed with an omelette.

"There's a boy in my daughter's life?"

"It's really nothing." Though thinking of Farouk in that moment was like taking a breath. My shoulders and my face relaxed.

"She always says that." Chloe closed her menu and put her chin in her palms like my mother had.

"Well, he's very smart. He's from the East Coast and he likes the beach," I said, eyes still on the menu.

"He's very cute. Tall, dark and handsome." Chloe wiggled her eyebrows.

"Those are the dangerous ones. The mysterious boys. They'll break your heart every time. Remember that, girls, a little maternal advice."

"He's not mysterious," I said. "He's just different."

"Has your dad met him?"

"No, Mother. Dad hasn't met him. And you're not going to meet him, because there's nothing serious." The waitress came to the table.

"How is your dad?" my mom said after we ordered.

"He's doing well. Busy at work."

"And Ruth?"

"She's fine. Working a lot too." I couldn't tell her about the baby. The words wouldn't come. I'd tell her the next time we talked on the phone. I had to prepare her for the news.

"How's cross-country? Preparing for varsity next year?"

I paused and Chloe looked at me. Her lips pressed together in a tight white line.

"Sam's been running her little feet off. Watched her meet the other day. She was trucking. She was a couple of steps behind the third-place girl. It was so awesome," said Chloe, just a little too loudly.

"See, you're getting there. Soon."

"Okay, enough, enough," Chloe said. "Tell us about big-city living." Chloe was nearly tipping the table as she leaned forward.

Chloe and my mom talked about San Francisco and Chloe promised to apply to Berkeley. I was relieved to have the pressure off me. I just couldn't tell my mom anything important. I was out of practice.

I tuned in to the conversation here and there, but I had nothing to add. I hadn't been up north, though my mom kept inviting me. I didn't want to leave my dad, and I wasn't sure I was ready to see the new wonderful life my mom had made without me.

"Time for presents," said Mom. She gave me a small pewter box with roses on the lid.

"For your earrings," she said.

"Thank you." I said. I didn't wear earrings. I put the box in my pocket. She gave Chloe a vanilla candle.

"For passion," she said.

"I hope to use it." Chloe held the candle to her nose and smiled at me.

After breakfast, we hugged and my mother left me just

as quickly as she'd come. As Chloe drove me home, I thought of running. I thought of the pattern of my breath as I hit my stride. I began to count to myself as Chloe played with the radio. I counted in fours because if I stopped, the tears in my eyes would spill over. I wouldn't be able to stop them.

Ruth and I shopped during the last days of the break. We went to different malls on days she told work she had doctors' appointments. We went to the baby section in department stores and she held up pajamas made to look like a tiny baseball uniform, or small jeans the same cut as the ones I was wearing.

Those clothes startled me. We could find the entire wardrobe of the popular girls at school. There were tiny tops meant to reveal a toddler's navel and pants that said CAPRI. How could anyone tell that a tiny baby's pants were shorter than normal?

"What eighteen-year-old fits into this?" said Ruth, holding up tiny crushed-velvet leggings and a halter top.

"Someone washed that in hot water, then returned it."

I would think at first how cute it was to dress a baby like that, but then about how uncomfortable those clothes were when I borrowed them from Chloe for our nights at the beach. Babies couldn't say that the lace itched their necks or that when the breeze blew, their tummies got cold.

Maybe Ruth thought these same things, because she only bought clothes for herself—overalls and crisp white shirts she could wear beneath a blazer, nothing that looked like maternity clothes.

She would turn in front of the store's mirror. "Is this at all flattering? Do I look like a stuffed turkey?" She'd smooth the front of a blazer and her belly would be defined.

"You look wonderful. Maternity is the new look for summer."

"Thank you, Samantha Pallas, *Vogue* editor." And then she'd shake her head and try on a different suit until she found one that made her look heavy and dowdy and not really pregnant.

"Try the first one again," I'd say, because I wanted her to be pregnant and wonderful and not wear those loose clothes like she had before—those clothes that turned my father off. Now she looked beautiful in a black sweater with a scoop neck so her pale skin glowed, and that was tight around her growing belly. She straightened her back and held her head up and she was one of those sexy women my dad wanted. But I didn't push it because I understood about keeping secrets. Maybe no one at work knew about the baby, but she wouldn't be able to keep the secret much longer.

I touched my stomach and turned to the side in the mirrors as she changed. I'd wear the sexy clothes if I were pregnant. I'd be beautiful and I wouldn't put up my hair like she did. I'd let it fall heavy and long across my back because it would shine and glow like hers. If I were pregnant, I wouldn't keep anything a secret anymore. I wouldn't have to because I would have someone in my life who didn't care about the things I didn't want other people to know.

• • •

On my first day back at school, I heard girls talking about Linda in my first-period class. She'd had the baby over break and had brought him to school to show everyone.

Linda was a big girl, and I couldn't remember her looking very pregnant. Perhaps, if Owen hadn't died, she would have been one of those girls on the news who hides her pregnancy the whole term, worried about her parents or her reputation, and then gives birth in a convenience store bathroom, only to leave the baby for someone else to find.

Between classes she stood in the hall with an infant in a little cap. He looked barely awake. She held him up and out like a shield. I hadn't ever been around a baby that small and soft, and it took my breath away that she held him like that above the cold tile covered in streaks from sneakers and clots of mud.

The warning bell rang, and I had one minute to make it to class. I hadn't moved. I wanted to hold that small, warm thing and take it with me outside the noisy hallway and lie with it in the grass somewhere and tell it all my secrets.

But I had to go before Linda saw me watching her and the baby. Some maternal instinct would tell her my thoughts.

I opened the door as the bell rang and it wasn't until I sat down and saw Farouk that I remembered it was math class. There he was in those grown-up clothes, khakis and a button-down shirt.

He ran his finger down my arm as I sat and I was irritated with him. I should have told him about his clothes before all of this happened. I should have told him to buy some surf trunks and flip-flops and to rub them around in the sand on some early morning when no one would be there to see him. I wanted him to fit in, perhaps to disappear, like I did.

"Did you get lost?" he said in his normal voice, and I looked around to see if people were looking at us. But they were talking to each other and holding brand-new bags and showing off new watches from Christmas.

"Chloe was in the hall," I said. I was wearing some gifts from my father. A blue silk hooded sweater and dark, nearly black jeans. He'd given me a new pair of running shoes, and shampoo and conditioner he must have bought at a salon, all very expensive. He wanted to give the best gifts, and when he opened his, he swore it was one of a kind. "I'll cherish it forever," he said, though it really was just another tie.

He gave Ruth a gold heart on a chain. He'd had something inscribed on the back and after Ruth read it, her eyes welled and she hugged him longer than I'd seen in months.

I looked closer at Farouk for his presents, but he didn't seem to have any. I hadn't noticed a Christmas tree at his house. I hadn't noticed any other religious things. I didn't know what he would celebrate or how.

"I never asked how your Christmas was," I said.

"Fine, more parties. I've worn out my Farsi."

"Yeah, I know what you mean. I've worn out my Swahili. And if I speak another word of Greek, I'm going to kill myself."

"Well, there's no need for that. We'll just speak in plain old English."

"Old English, like Shakespeare?"

"Thou art very funny, Sam."

The teacher said, "Farouk, what did you do on your break?"

The class quieted and the tips of my ears burned. I dropped my shoulders and let my hair fall over my face because I could feel people looking through me to see what the new boy would say.

"San Diego is where we used to come on vacation. So I still consider this a vacation even though we live here. I checked out the beaches and Coronado and just tried to find my way around." I expected someone to groan or make a face or laugh. That was the wrong answer. Only people with pale legs and T-shirts that said SAN DIEGO came here on vacation and enjoyed it. He should not have admitted that he wasn't from here. But no one laughed or made a face and some weren't even paying attention.

The teacher continued calling on people to share what they did on their breaks and the surfer girl behind me described skiing in Utah.

A girl in the back corner who I'd forgotten was even in the class said she'd gone to Africa. I didn't believe her. Small blond girls like her did not go to Africa. They stayed in their small room and read books about Africa so they could tell their class with a trace of a newly acquired accent that they had been to faraway places.

If the teacher had called on me, I would have made something up too. I couldn't say that I spent my break sleeping in late, and going to bed early and waiting for the boy who was sitting next to me to throw pebbles at my window and take me away to his dark house, where he would show me maps in carpets and the ancient stories they told.

But she did not call on me and the only time I moved after she started the class was to hand in my homework. I tipped the paper toward Farouk as I handed it up because I wanted him to see what happened when he wasn't there to help. There was a problem I had almost solved. The numbers were working at each step and it felt like I was on the right track, but I didn't finish it just in case I was wrong the whole time.

I found Chloe in the quad staring at Linda as she handed the baby to the girls who used to be Owen's friends. Chloe didn't turn away until I sat and said her name twice.

"She named the kid Owen." She rolled her eyes. "How trashy can you get? That name sucks, dead dad or not." She grabbed my arm and stood. We walked past the quad and out toward the track and football field.

"I'm sure the Killgores are happy about it," I said. The mural of smiling students on the side of a building seemed freshly painted. The rainbow of shirts and skin tones looked new and hopeful.

"I don't even think it's his. The skin is too dark to be Owen. The kid doesn't even have rosy cheeks." She shook her head.

"Babies that little only look like other babies that little," I said. But the baby had Linda's perfectly round face and wide-open eyes.

"She's such a slut, who can really tell?" said Chloe.

"Why are you so pissed?" I said. "Be happy. Now the Killgores have something to distract them from Owen's death."

We were at the field. The track was raked, ready for the

teams to practice. The green grass of the football field held bright white lines for the afternoon games.

"I'm mad because she lives there. She eats dinner with them every night. She takes advantage," said Chloe. She let go of my arm and sat at the top of the concrete bleachers.

I thought it sounded like a good deal. The Killgores got a brand-new Owen, and Linda got a family to take care of him. She had a baby, but now she was free to leave him with them. When she grew tired of this small thing she didn't know how to hold, she could leave him with the Killgores. And the price they all paid seemed too small to me. I was sure that Henry did not mind escaping Owen's shadow, and the boys on the team were happy to be recognized for their own talents. And Owen's parents had a chance to start over again with a fresh baby, to try out all the things they had learned from their mistakes. They could change and have a boy who wouldn't kill himself in the middle of the night despite all he had.

I hadn't gotten my period since that night with Farouk. It wasn't yet time, but if I was pregnant, I didn't think I would have wanted to stay at his house and become part of his family. The baby and I would be swallowed whole into the rugs and the mess. And I didn't think Farouk's father felt like he had made any mistakes.

"Maybe they want to be taken advantage of," I said. I stretched my back and put my feet on the bleacher in front of me. I bent forward to stretch the back of my legs. I hadn't run all break; I hadn't run seriously for two months. I moved close to Chloe to keep warm. Could my muscles forget in that amount of time? Had they dissolved? I had chosen Farouk over running, but it seemed like a very right choice.

"Let her have them," I said. "Think about her own parents, and how they gave her up so easily. Would you want parents like that?"

"I have parents like that," she said. She reached in a pocket of her jacket and took out a cigarette. She lit it as I watched her. I realized that I was not talking about Linda's parents, but about my own.

My mother had easily given me up to my father, who she knew hadn't changed from the man who would tell her he was going away on business and just stay around the corner in his girlfriend's apartment. She knew I would be alone. She'd said she needed a new life. She didn't need to say that it didn't include me.

My father easily gave me up each time he asked me to lie for him. To be an alibi. But unlike Linda's parents, my family didn't leave me with people who were more capable than they were. My parents left me with myself, trusting that at some point they had been good parents. That, in a moment of excellent parenting, they had taught me what I needed to know. But all I could think was that I still made it to school each day and got passing grades despite their bad parenting.

"My dad is like that," said Chloe, and I had to replay her words in my head to make sure I hadn't said them. She handed the cigarette to me and I inhaled deeply, more deeply than I had in the past because then I had worried about my lungs. But with Chloe that afternoon, the smoke felt good. The smoke choked just a little, like running had.

"I think that's just how dads are," I said. She put her arm through mine.

"Your dad's cool," she said. The bell rang in the distance.

"You can have him," I said, and we waited for the warning bell to ring. I was daydreaming about giving my father away, about giving him to Chloe to show her that I was right about all dads.

"C'mon, Sammy. They're going to miss us." She stood.

"The whole school would fall apart if we didn't show up," I said as we walked back through the buildings and past the locker room. A girl pushed open the door to the locker room and I tried to peek in, to make sure things were the same, to make sure I hadn't missed anything. As we walked I pictured it, the best runners breathing to a count of four and the coach clapping her hands about one of the best girl's grades, or a rival team losing a meet and dropping out of our rank.

I was a girl with a boy who loved me, and if I went inside I would be sucked back in and transformed into that invisible girl I once had been.

"Tell your teacher you hurt your ankle at lunch and that you just got done in the nurse's office," said Chloe as she left me in front of her class. I hugged her and for a moment I wanted to cry because I hadn't hugged anybody so hard in so long. I was supposed to get this satisfaction from Farouk, and no one else, but then I pushed that idea away and felt grateful that there were so many people who wanted to touch me.

I began to walk away from Chloe and she called, "Limp, for God's sake." She opened the door to her classroom.

I limped until I knew she couldn't see me and then I walked normally into class.

• • •

After school, my stomach was cold with anticipation for my afternoon with Farouk. He was waiting for me in his usual spot near the teachers' cars.

He sat in his car and he didn't hug me or take my hand when I sat. He was waiting until we were alone, away from school, so I didn't touch him first. I could wait.

"I need to take you straight home," he said as he started the engine.

"Okay," I said. I hadn't been home early, alone, in months. What would I do with that time?

"My grandfather arrived last night. He would tell my dad that I wasn't home," he said.

And I relaxed some, but not completely. I needed an excuse for Ruth in case she was home.

"You must be excited to have him here. A grandparent to spoil you for a little while," I said, smiling, so he would see that I was not bothered about having our afternoon taken from me.

"I am," he said, and he nodded as if convincing himself. "I'm glad, but he'll comment on my Farsi. He'll say something about the American food we eat."

I wondered if the man would bring new smells with him. If he would change the makeup of the house, if the messes would be cleaned and the rugs sorted through and the best chosen for him to admire and remember.

Each time Farouk turned a corner I held on tighter than I needed to, hoping that instead of going left or right, he would make a U-turn and take me someplace new. But he stopped at my house and cut the engine as we sat.

Without the heat on, his car cooled quickly.

"Thanks for the ride," I said. He nodded and we were quiet for a minute more. I knew I should get out of the car, but I began talking. I couldn't help it.

"The boy who died, Owen Killgore. His girlfriend Linda brought their baby to school today. Chloe didn't think it was his. But I'm not sure," I said, and shook my head like I was thinking what a shame it was that teenagers got into such trouble. But I was thinking of what I could say next, what would keep me in this car despite the cool metal and the glass steaming from my breath. "I think Owen's parents want it to be his so bad that they don't look close, but who knows, maybe she only had sex with him. Maybe she wasn't a slut like everyone thought she was." I took a breath, but it didn't feel like I got the oxygen I needed to continue, to make my heart keep pounding as fast as it was.

"Sam, I really need to go. We can have lunch tomorrow and you can finish the story," he said, and put his hand on my arm. He looked at me and squinted like Ruth had done some winter mornings last year when I told her I was sick because I simply didn't want to go to school.

"I just think there is something wrong with the whole thing and I wanted to talk about it," I said. Words kept coming out of me, and I wasn't sure what I was saying. I couldn't hear myself.

I thought I could tell him that I hadn't gotten my period yet. That each morning I touched my belly like Ruth did so often. How I stood up from my bed and crossed slowly to the bathroom hoping that in the night the cells that needed to divide and multiply would have done what they needed and thinking that if I walked slowly enough everything would stay where it was and there would be no blood in my underwear. I knew it was crazy. I knew I'd be like Linda, not sure how to hold or touch the baby. But I wanted to act scared when I told him so he would comfort me. So he would take me inside and pull the hair from my eyes and lay me down on my bed. And I would get him to have sex with me again just to increase my chances of being pregnant. If I were pregnant, a new pocket inside me would open and in that small dark place I would feel full. Though as I sat in his car and touched my stomach again I knew there was nothing in there. There was no baby.

Farouk leaned over and kissed my cheek and I knew I had pushed it too far. I blushed, embarrassed about those empty words that floated all around us, and wanted to apologize, but any more would make him turn on me. So I opened the door and stepped out. I shut the door and waved and walked behind his car so he could drive away without having to make sure I got in the house safely.

I waited for someone to come home, sitting at the table with my hands flat on the glass, watching the fog grow on the glass around my fingers. I opened a book for school and read a paragraph over and over. I considered calling Chloe, but I worried that I would talk again like I had talked with Farouk and my secrets would slip out.

The garage door opened. I picked up a pen and smoothed a white sheet of paper and pressed the book flat. But my hands were shaking. I expected Ruth to walk up the stairs and tell me stories about her day, about a strange new thing her body or the baby was doing. My father appeared.

I stared for a second, not recognizing him and wondering who this man was in my house.

"I didn't expect you here," he said. He looked calm, but his eyes were smudged with purple.

"I didn't expect you, either." I pressed my hand against the cool glass to calm myself. The glass table was slick with the sweat from my hand.

"I came home to take a nap, have some quiet time," he said. I had surprised him. I wasn't where I should have been, where he was counting on me to be. I wanted to close my eyes like I had when I was a child, hiding from my parents. "If you can't see them, they can't see you," my mom said.

"I'm just studying; I won't disturb you." But I already had. I'd broken a small unspoken agreement.

"I'm going to sleep, so I won't disturb you, either," he said. He moved over to me and looked at the book.

"I read that one in college. I'll help you with the essay," he said, and put his hand on top of my head. He made a fist and hit it with his other hand, then ran his hand down my hair.

"Did it feel like an egg cracking?" he said, and tugged on my braid.

"I really thought I was going to have to take a shower," I said, and now everything was okay. He was all right with my being home so early. He forgave me for being someplace I shouldn't have been.

He walked up the stairs to his room and I listened for his sounds. The closet door hitting the wall with a small thud. His footsteps on the floor above me. And I tried to figure out the difference between these new sounds and Ruth's sounds, which were always quieter and faster, like she was making a secret getaway.

The phone rang and I jumped up to answer, but my dad had already gotten it. I picked up just in case it was Farouk, just in case he called often and my father never left me the message. As I picked up I heard a woman greet my dad, but he was quiet. He was listening for me and she was silent. I hung up. I stood beneath the stairs listening, wanting him to call down the stairs for me that my teacher was on the line, or my mother.

After a few moments, my father opened his closet and wandered around his room. The toilet flushed and water ran in the sink and finally his door opened again. I went back to my seat and put my hands on the icy glass.

My father came down in chinos and a shirt that had been pressed and hung in a dry-cleaning bag. His skin was clear and his cheeks pink, like he had rested all afternoon.

"Don't spend it all in one place," he said, and handed me a twenty.

"Big spender." I crumpled the bill in my palm.

"Ruth will be home soon; you guys get dinner. Don't make her cook," he said.

"You look good, Dad, coming home early becomes you."

"You look tired, Sam. Rest and tell Ruth that a client called. We're having a meeting."

"I'll tell her a woman called. She won't be surprised; she won't even be hurt," I said, sure that Ruth had been hurt in the past. That she was used to the late nights, the emergency meetings. She worked with him, she would know which clients were in town and needed attention.

"Tell her whatever you want, but you'll be the one having to explain to her why your story is different than mine."

He straightened his shoulders and pulled his sleeves to

his wrists. I'd watched him do this in the mirror before going to work in the morning. It was his last moment to make sure he looked perfect—as handsome as he knew he was.

"You look good, Dad," I said. "Your clients will be impressed by your casual yet professional presentation." I slid my hands off the table and scraped my palms hard over the glass edge.

"That's what I like to hear," he said, and kissed the top of my head. My hands smarted and I made fists to keep that cold, burning feeling inside them.

"Are they all like you?" I asked him as he turned away from me.

And he didn't even stop. Not even a pause to consider what he should tell his daughter. The girl sitting in a dark, cold room, home at a time she shouldn't be. He didn't even turn.

"All of them," he said. And he jogged down the stairs to the garage and his car.

All he had to do was open the garage door and press the gearshift into reverse and be gone. I had nowhere to go. I had barely been beyond the eastern edges of San Diego.

Maybe he'd answered me correctly. Perhaps he thought I'd meant businesspeople, or grown-ups or men who were trapped with a pregnant girlfriend.

I meant the boys on the beach and Owen and his friends, and Farouk. I hoped that maybe my father was running late and he didn't have time to explain to me that boys must learn this behavior. They have to fall in love once and be very much in love and then realize there are many people they can love like that, and many who will love them in return. Over the years they will discover that it's worth the lies and the guilt to have many women they can love. Maybe I still had time to be that first love for some of them and then *I* could be done with *them* before they found the others.

I closed my eyes and rested my forehead on the cool table and wished that I would be that girl for Farouk. I made a deal with whoever would listen that I would give him up so he could learn to be like my father as soon as it was time. As soon as he loved me more than he would love anyone else in his life, even if he found others.

I promised it over and over until the garage door opened again and Ruth came up the stairs calling to me to help her with the groceries she planned to cook for me and for my father, who had promised her earlier in the day that he would be home for dinner just this one night.

chapter eleven

I got my period the next day. It was the middle of the night and I had been dreaming of Farouk. He wore an army uniform and his lips were pink as if he'd just rubbed lipstick from them. And I knew as I woke it was my lipstick he had rubbed away. In those moments as I woke and wondered why I was waking, I was happy. I had been kissing those lips again. Kissing in a quiet room with deep red carpets on the walls.

I put my hand over my face to stop myself from waking completely. I wanted those moments to stay with me, to hold me over into another dream. But my legs felt sticky and I lay for a second longer, holding my breath, asking my body to keep whatever it was inside me from spilling out. I wanted that hope that I could keep a small piece of Farouk.

I sat up slowly and walked to the bathroom in the dark, savoring each bit of the dream before I turned the light on and sat down.

There was no baby, and I searched my underwear and the toilet and the sheets, though I'd known all along I'd never have the control my mother had when she was determined to have me. And I went to bed with clean sheets and I closed my eyes. I fell into sleep quickly, though this time I didn't dream. When I woke in the morning I searched my memories of the night for another dream I could take with me to school and play during classes when I missed Farouk, but there were none.

He still gave me a few rides home, but each time he drove me straight from school to my house. He was quiet in the car.

"I'm feeling better about math," I'd said one day, not because I really was, but because he hadn't said more than two words to me since we'd left the school. His knuckles were white as he gripped the steering wheel.

"I'm happy."

"I love this song." I patted my thighs along with the jazz coming from the speakers.

"I don't know it."

I didn't know it either, though I kept tapping.

"Chloe thinks she failed a Spanish test today." He nodded and rubbed the bridge of his nose. He couldn't find his way through the condos too quickly. The car lurched as he pulled in front of my door.

"All right," he said. It was time for me to get out, and I

was ready to go. I was embarrassed that I couldn't keep quiet. And this was how his rides went. I talked, he nodded. I regretted taking the ride.

And then the rides stopped.

It was in math that Farouk touched my arm. He hadn't touched me in days. I tried to be still, but I began to shake, my muscles tense from the effort.

"I can't take you home today," he said. "My grandfather ran out of medication. We need to take him to the doctor to make sure he's okay. It's my fault, I should have spent more time with him. I would have known he'd run out and hadn't been taking it."

"It's not your fault. He's a doctor," I said. "Can't he just prescribe himself some?" I had been taking notes on the numbers on the board. It was a section I understood. They were travel problems. Problems measuring speed and distance. I was happy to solve them a second before the teacher.

"Very nice," he said, and looked away from me. I continued taking notes, though when he wouldn't talk to me again and he didn't look over to see if I was making the right marks, I wanted to apologize. If I could have taken it back, I would have. I would have swallowed all my frustration at his being distant each afternoon.

Math class ended and Farouk didn't ask me if I'd be okay without a ride home. He left before I had even gathered my bag and my books and let the people behind push past me out the door. When I was finally out the halls had cleared and Farouk was gone.

I was able to focus on my next class. I simply listened to what the teacher said and wrote down the points I would need to know. I was able to stay clear because I told myself that math class hadn't happened and that I would get a ride home in a nice car with a boy in an ironed shirt.

Chloe waited for me during lunch. She sat alone in a shady corner near my class. She watched Linda in the center of the quad laughing with the popular girls. Linda's belly was still swollen from pregnancy, but no one cared that she was fat. They wanted to hold the baby that she brought more days than not. And she was getting better with the baby. She held him close to her and pressed a hat on his head.

"See that blanket?" said Chloe. "It's from Notre Dame. He wanted to go there since he was a kid, but he nearly flunked English, junior year. Who flunks English? He had to take a summer class, but it was too late. Permanent record. She's such an idiot. I'd do a better job."

"Well, you can prove yourself at my house soon. Ruth's having a baby."

"She is?" Chloe sat up. "Congratulations!" She pinched my shoulder. "You'll be a sister."

"You can be an auntie."

"When?"

"Soon. A couple more months before the little monster pops out. I couldn't tell you because Dad and Ruth wanted to keep it a secret."

"I can't wait." She clapped her hands and rested her head on my shoulder again.

"I'm happy," she whispered.

"Me too."

• • •

One afternoon, Chloe had the car. The final bell had rung and the school was nearly empty. The basketball team jogged past us, doing laps around the school. The team was short and scrawny and the leader ran more slowly than the slowest girl on cross-country. They were out of breath by the quad.

"Don't those guys work out every day after school?" I said. "How are they such crappy runners?"

"Show them what's up."

"Next time," I said as they began the slight hill to the track field.

"Let's go to the mall. We'll try on prom dresses and wedding dresses. You'll be my bridesmaid," Chloe said.

"As long as you promise that I'll always be the bridesmaid and never the bride."

"You'll have many opportunities to get it on with the best man. I plan to be married at least ten times."

Chloe put her arm through mine and we walked away from the school and toward the office and out into the nearly empty parking lot. I saw Chloe's car in a spot far away, and Farouk's car close. He was leaning against it talking to a girl with the same coloring he had. She was a year older so I didn't know her name. But I'd seen her after school earlier in the year waiting for her boyfriend to pick her up on Friday afternoons in his black convertible. Her car would be the last in the lot as I finished cross-country practice. Its red paint baked in the sun and once I caught her climbing out of her boyfriend's car, her hair pulled up in a knotted ponytail and her heavy gold jewelry tangled in the palm of her hand. Her face was bare and her lips pink and she was beautiful. She kissed her boyfriend again and he drove away before she had even started her own car.

I watched Farouk and that girl talk and the two of them looked like adults. Farouk wore a pressed shirt and she wore women's clothes—a suit and pointed shoes with a delicate heel. She didn't stand too close to him and he didn't touch her and so I simply watched. I didn't feel jealousy or anger like I had during math class when he talked to the surfer girl in the seat behind me.

Chloe stood next to me and saw them too. She must have sensed that I was not upset and so she didn't call the girl a bitch or a slut.

I walked toward them and Chloe followed and we were quiet. I didn't want to interrupt them; I just wanted to know what two grown-up-looking kids would have to say to each other. And so we walked past them, his back to us so he never noticed how close I got. How I could smell his warm pepper smell. At first I tried to make out what they said. After we had walked beyond them I understood that Farouk was speaking a different language. His breathy vowels and syllables sounded the same as those in his name.

And they could have been talking about anything, about the weather, or classes or the stupid white kids at the school. But to me, when I played those words over in my mind, they were telling stories of faraway places and great sadness. And this is what I wanted to think. I wanted to believe that Farouk had found someone who would understand him. Who would believe that there were magical places far beyond California. I was relieved because it meant that he would spend more time with me and he wouldn't be frustrated that I didn't understand. He wouldn't try to tell me, he would just kiss me and lie on top of me and take my breath away with his weight. And then he could call this girl or take her to lunches and tell her his thoughts that I didn't understand.

He didn't see us as we passed him. Chloe opened the passenger door for me.

"Are you moving on?" she asked.

The air was cold, but the bright sun was shining. I knew that the inside of Farouk's car would be hot and dry and that I would have sat in there until I ran out of oxygen just to be warm and smell that old-leather smell.

"I'm not doing anything," I said.

"I've seen him with that Persian girl before. He goes off campus with her group for lunch," she said. I shivered and my stomach began to burn.

"His grandfather's in town. Maybe their families know each other," I said. She went around to her side and opened the door. We both got in. Her car was warm too. It smelled like vanilla.

"I'm sure they do," said Chloe. She started the engine and drove the long way out of school so I wouldn't have to look at them again. "Or maybe you're way better than he is."

"I doubt it." I ran my thumb down the warm glass of the window. A girl ran down into the canyon where I had met Owen that day. She shouldn't have been alone.

"I don't," she said, and floored it through a yellow light.

"The families know each other from Iran. The rich people there stick together. They marry each other to keep the money. And especially because of the revolution," I said. And I continued to make up stories about Iran. Stories that I was sure Farouk would have told me eventually. I told Chloe anything I thought of to make sense of his lies or

Chloe's gossip or my own naiveté. I talked while we drove and as we walked into the mall.

"Sounds complicated," said Chloe, and she let me talk, though I think she had just stopped listening. I could feel her pulling away and believing less of what I had to say. But if I continued talking I would hit on the truth eventually.

The next day, when the final bell rang, I walked to the library. I saw Farouk walking to his car, but I kept my eyes straight ahead. I didn't wave to him or say goodbye. I wanted to look like I was going to the library to study for a big test or to do extra homework that I had accepted just for the challenge of it. And he didn't look at me, either. He looked toward his car in the parking lot and once he looked down and smoothed the front of his shirt beneath the strap of his backpack.

And so I waited in the library and touched the spines of books that I should have read long ago to make myself smart, to keep up with him. Perhaps if I had read them I would have been in more of his classes. I could have taught him things, impressed him with my understanding of how the world worked. Physics and biology. But there hadn't been time. I couldn't have known that Owen would die on the same day a new boy would arrive and be for me what Owen had been for the whole school. I took a science book from the shelf and pressed each of the magnified red blood cells pictured on the cover.

Inside, the print was small and the photos were grainy black and white. And I was grateful that they were hazy because the blurry photos of human hearts and lungs and kidneys were enough to make me queasy. There was a whole section on the development of a baby and I found the size of Ruth's near the end of the cycle. And it was a real baby, not like the small marine creatures in the early months. This little baby was ready to be born. Its fingers and nose seemed close enough to Linda's baby and I thought there was no reason for Ruth's baby to stay in her longer than that moment. She should tell her doctor to hurry things along so that she would have the baby before my father left completely. She should have it while he was still there at least one night a week for a quick dinner before he left for a run in the night or to play racquetball in the condo's courts.

I sat with that book turning pages and bringing my face close to the photos until, like clouds, they blurred into something not scary or sickening but sweet and necessary like rain on the ocean or wet leaves. And I waited until after I knew everyone would be gone to leave the library, to walk home the long way through the twisting streets of different condo complexes. Each time I felt lost, I recognized a building from the time I ran this way to get far, far away from Owen Killgore.

He sat away from me in math class. He sat close to the front, near a popular boy who appeared in skateboarding magazines. Chloe had had a crush on that boy in ninth grade.

Farouk sat there with his feet on the chair in front of him and talked to that boy like he'd been sitting there the whole school year. I overheard Farouk describing skate parks on the East Coast and I cringed. He was telling too much. No one would care about places they'd never been and people they didn't know. And the boy listened and nodded and laughed at things that I didn't think were funny. Class began, and Farouk didn't look over this boy's shoulder to make sure he understood everything.

I walked home after spending nearly an hour in the library looking at books and reading the words in a whisper, trying to understand or even just to focus from the start of the sentence to the finish. I thought those books would help me in math class. I would be a more logical person because I understood why a mouse and a rat were not as closely related as people thought. But even this I was unsure of. And none of those books helped me to pay attention when Farouk stopped looking at me altogether. When he stopped lifting his head in a short nod as he passed me in the halls or on his way to his car, I tried to think of biology and nature and the way animals worked, but all I could see was that for him, I had stopped existing. I had merely disappeared. And I thought that I would have to look disappearance up in one of those books just to make sure that it couldn't really happen to a real human being.

Chloe and I sat against the wall and watched the rest of the school move and laugh and talk. Finally, one day was bright and clear and there was no breeze to chill me through my sweatshirt. It was like the day Owen had died.

"Maybe his heart really did swell up." She had sensed the day was like Owen's last day and Farouk's first.

"It's possible," I said, watching the crowd. I still looked for Farouk, but I never thought I would ever really see him again.

"Maybe there's a metaphor in it all somewhere," she said.

"Maybe," I said, though I disagreed. I had accepted Owen's suicide. As I watched Linda with that baby I thought that he must have known that the two of them together would have been worse than just one parent who had no idea what to do with this new little thing.

Or maybe Owen had the first case of disappearing. He had somehow contracted it from another person. Maybe one of the boys who beat him in that last race gave it to him. Or willed it onto Owen to make him lose. And then Owen passed it to me and I would pass it to Chloe.

And as I drifted through school and didn't have to pay attention in class or do my homework I thought it wouldn't be all bad. I thought that I could live my whole life this way. And that if it got worse, I could be close again to Farouk without his ever knowing.

But then Ruth went into labor early. I came home one afternoon from school and found her note.

Sam, it read. *The baby is coming! A friend from work is taking me to the hospital, and Dad is meeting me there. The pain isn't so bad, so don't worry. I know you're worrying, but stop. Stop now. Okay? Now, do some homework and get your final full night of sleep. Soon you'll be a sister. I love you, Ruth.*

I went downstairs to get her car. It was there, but there were no keys. I searched the junk drawers for a spare key, but all I found were exhausted batteries and screwdrivers, and knotted ribbon for gift-wrap. I called my father. His secretary said he had gone home and that I should try there. I told her thank you and hung up.

And so I dialed that number that was so familiar, but oddly twisted and rearranged, and I waited for Farouk to answer. But it was an old man who said what it took me a few seconds to understand as hello.

I asked for Farouk.

"Farouk no," said the man, and he hung up. I was lowering the phone when I heard "Sam," in a whisper.

"Hello," I said, and pressed the receiver to my ear.

"What do you need?" Farouk whispered.

"I need a ride," I said. "Ruth is having the baby."

He was quiet; then he said, "Okay. I'll be right there," and he hung up.

I dumped the books from my backpack and ran up the stairs to Ruth's room and packed the bag with the first underwear I grabbed and I pulled shirts from her closet and a pair of pajamas. And I wasn't sure what she would need. So I packed whatever would fit, never thinking that she might have already done this. That she had expected all along to go into labor and need to stay in a hospital.

When the bag was bulging, I went downstairs and sat on the dusty couch no one ever sat on and I waited for Farouk to arrive. Maybe I should go back upstairs because he might throw rocks again. Or maybe I should go outside because he would honk from the street.

He knocked on the front door. I answered it with the backpack over my shoulder and the smell of Ruth's clothes surrounding me.

"Thank you for helping me," I said.

"Where are we going?"

She'd told me, I was sure. I tried to think, was it one of the university hospitals? There were two. One right up the road, and one miles away. And then there was the hospital with the stork that watched over the freeway from the parking garage. Could that one be it? But I think the last time I drove by, there was construction.

"I'm not sure," I said. "How do I find out?" Maybe his doctor's instinct would help us. The bag was growing heavy on my shoulder. I stepped toward the door, hoping we could begin looking for her.

"Why didn't she tell you?" He was still standing outside. I knew that I should bring him in and lock the door so he couldn't leave again. I could call the different hospitals while he sat at the table and waited. Maybe I wouldn't find her and he would have to sit there. He'd have to be with me.

"Sam, why didn't she tell you?" And I understood the question. I understood that he wasn't asking me out of irritation with Ruth. He was asking me like a teacher would turn to the class and ask why she had put a particular number in the equation. She knew the answer, and the rest of the class knew and I was truly waiting for why she put the number there. But with Farouk standing there, I knew the answer before someone else gave it.

"I thought she would want me there."

"You're not family. There's nothing you can do. You'd sit in the waiting room."

"She's alone."

"Your dad will be there," he said.

"I don't think so. He wasn't at work and he wasn't picking up his cell phone."

"He's probably already there."

I dropped the bag and backed away from the door to let him in. But he stood watching me. And I thought that maybe my father was there, but I didn't feel better knowing he was there and hadn't called me. He hadn't come by to pick me up. There was nothing for me to do at the hospital.

"Come in," I said.

"I'm going home," Farouk said.

"Come in."

The tile in front of the door felt like a cavern. And still Farouk stood.

"No more, Sam," he said.

"I don't understand," I said.

"I have other things to do," he said.

"I'm here." My voice was louder than it needed to be.

"You're crazy," he said, and stepped onto the tile in the house. He smiled as he said it and pressed his thumb into my temple. And he kissed me on my mouth and on my cheek. As he pulled away, I knew that he would never see me again.

"Asheghetam, lakpost," he said, and turned away and walked back to his car.

"I don't understand," I said, though I could hear him getting into his car. I heard the low rumble and the start of the engine.

I saw those words in my head. The soft *a* and the smooth *m*. I tried rearranging the sounds so they meant something very important, but there was nothing. I stood letting the cool, moist air into the house and I thought that like an echo, the meaning would come back on the wind.

• • •

I fell asleep on the couch and dreamt dreams of colors like splattered paint and Lava lamps. The phone rang.

"Kid," my dad whispered.

"Dad!"

"We had a boy. He's perfect. But not nearly as perfect as you are." He still whispered. His words had a breathlessness I hadn't heard before. He was amazed.

"Is Ruth okay?"

"She's wonderful. Very brave."

"I wanted to be there."

"I'll bring you first thing tomorrow. Ruth is sleeping, so you should too. Ruth loves you and I love you."

"I love you guys, too. Tell the baby I love him, too."

I did what my dad had told me to do. I slept again, this time without dreams. My mind was still and dark, and in the morning I was grateful.

chapter twelve

Ruth brought the baby home after a few days. My dad had been there for her. He'd gotten to the hospital as she was giving birth and he'd caught the baby as he came out. When I first saw them at the hospital, Ruth held her baby like he was supposed to be held, close to her heart. She kissed his head and smelled his little neck and they named him after my grandfather. Ernest. It was an old man's name.

"That would be a good name to live up to," I said. I held his tiny red fingers in mine. He had a full head of black hair.

"He will. You're his big sister; you'll make sure." She put her arm around me and held us both tight.

"I will. I promise," I said, not knowing at all how I would do that.

My father assembled baby furniture and filled their room with a crib and changing table. He was home after work, too. He came home promptly and used regular laundry detergent to wash Ernest's clothes and he pressed diapers on too tight. And Ruth let him do all these things, but when he would leave the room, she'd whisper to me, "Sam, Sam."

"This is how you cut the blood circulation to a baby's legs." She tried wedging a finger between the diaper and my brother's leg. Ernest stared up at her, his eyes still a deep blue. He watched her as she laughed and she tore off the diaper.

"I'll do it," I said. She stepped aside but he continued to watch her as I reattached the diaper so it was tight enough, but not so tight he got red marks.

"One day we'll come home and the poor kid won't have any legs at all," she said, laughing.

"Maybe we should buy larger diapers."

"Maybe we should find a new diaper changer," she said, and put her hand over her mouth. "Did I say that?"

"I'll never tell."

She nursed in a rocking chair she'd made my dad bring from her storage space.

"I was nursed in this chair," she said. It was thick with glossy white paint. I sat next to her as she looked down at my brother and hummed. Ernest's eyes were closed and his mouth beginning to relax. He would wake with a start if she pulled away, so she let him sleep there, milk dribbling down his chin.

She looked at me. "Sam, what happened to the boy in the Jaguar?"

I shook my head. "Nothing. He just doesn't take me home anymore."

She lifted Ernest up and put him to her shoulder. He sighed and kept sleeping. She patted his back.

With her free hand she pulled my chair close to hers. She rubbed my cheek with her thumb, and then patted my shoulders like she patted my brother's.

"I'm sorry, honey," she said.

I nodded again and there was no number I could count to to stop from crying.

Ruth began to leave for an hour here, two hours there. She didn't say where she was going, though I didn't think to ask. And in her absence Ernest was usually quiet. He watched the ceiling, waiting like the rest of us for her to return and bring noise and warmth back to the house.

I slept less, listening in the night to his cries and Ruth's low murmuring. Sometimes that would put me back to sleep too, but if I couldn't sleep and if I heard my dad in the kitchen heating a bottle, I went down to keep him company as the milk warmed.

"Babies," he said. "This takes me way back. You'd think after all this time, babies would have evolved to sleep better."

Outside the kitchen window, the houses glowed blue in

the night. Windows were dark and dew covered the cars in gray gauze. My dad took the bottle out of the hot water and squirted a drop on his wrist.

"Perfect," he said.

"Quite the professional," I said, proud of him.

"It's like riding a bike. Plus, I was the one in charge of bottles with you. Mom always heated them too fast and you'd get gas. Nothing's really changed."

"You're a laugh riot."

"Go to bed, kid. Your work is done here," he said as he turned off the stove.

"He's worth it," I said.

"He is," said my dad.

The house was warm. Ruth had turned on the heat and I didn't need a sweatshirt; Ruth's cheeks were always pink. When I had a moment alone with Ernest, I would hold him tight to my chest and smell the top of his head.

"Hello, Ernest. My brother. It's your sister," I would say. "Sis."

He'd reach his hand up and my hair would tangle in his hot fingers.

"Sis," I'd say again, letting my breath come out in a whistle from my teeth, and he would smile.

And when I thought I'd cry from so much happiness, I would put him back in his bassinet, and think of Farouk and how much better I would feel with something of his close to me. Something I could smell and touch that would remind me of a time when I thought I was the thing Farouk would love the most.

My mom called and as I answered I heard Ernest crying. I knew my mom could hear it.

"Ruth had a baby," I said. It was easy to say after the months of keeping it in. He cried, and I knew it was his hungry cry. It was time for him to be fed.

"I know," she said. "Your dad told me. I'm happy for her. I'm happy for you."

"How long have you known?"

"Awhile. I thought you'd tell me in your own time. And you did." Ernest cried more and Ruth began singing to him. He quieted.

"I like having him around."

"Babies are great. Kids are great. Like you. Send me a picture of the little guy."

"I will," I said. I sent her a picture Ruth had taken of me holding him with a bottle to his lips. And she sent me a picture back. It was orange and curling around the edges. It was my mom holding me. She smiled as I reached up, tangling my hand in her long hair.

As Ernest grew, his skin lost the red glow and faded to a pink, so pale and clear. The days began to warm up. I still wore jeans to school but by lunch I would take my sweatshirt off. Chloe and I sat on the grass in a quiet part of the school lawn. She pulled up her sleeves, put on her sunglasses, and lay back squinting at the sky. The cuts on her arms were small notches, little scratches over the fading scars of longer and deeper cuts. I didn't have to ask her what was wrong, because now she told me when her brother was in town, or when she found her mother at the kitchen table, her face pale and still, with tears dripping from her chin.

"It's my dad's fault. Total neglect. It's a miracle I came out okay," she said as we lay there with the grass cushioning our backs.

"But why cut yourself? He'll never see it. He'll never beg you to stop."

"You're right, but I can't believe he would leave us like this. I can't believe he won't help my brother," she said to the sky.

"They're all like that," I said. I had learned my lesson. I was not surprised anymore when I watched Farouk put his hand on the Persian girl's back on their way to class. I watched, knowing the feeling of that hand on my back. Watching was all I could do.

But Chloe had faith that someone in this world would love her the best and never leave her alone with something sharp so she could cut her skin.

One day, right after my brother sat up without help for just a second, I came home and all of Ruth's absences made sense.

I was hot and sunburned after walking home and my father startled me as I walked in the door.

He was sitting on the couch I had sat on to wait for Farouk that last time. My father sat with his palms pressed together and his skin gray like he had been sick.

"Why are you here?" I said.

"Ruth's gone."

"I'm here now, you can go back to work. I'll watch the

baby," I said. I thought he must be upset because he was missing something very important at work.

"She moved," he said. "She moved out."

"What do you mean?"

"She's gone. Ruth and Ernest are gone."

I stared at him. My knees locked and my fists curled at my sides. "What did you finally do? What was it that finally forced her to leave?"

"Nothing. I was here. You've seen me here."

"Dad, Dad. You're such a jerk. You were a few years too late."

I ran up the stairs and my father followed me. I ran past my room to theirs. All the baby furniture was gone. The bed was made and the walls bare. The closet doors clean and shut. For a moment I was crazy enough to hope that Ruth had simply moved the baby and that she would be back to inhabit this bare space.

"She found a condo near here," he said.

"A condo. She *had* a condo." My heart was beating so loudly in my ears, I wasn't sure I'd heard him right.

"She got a new one."

My breathing grew deeper, and my heart felt like it would shake my ribs. That was what she had been doing in those hours away. She was searching for her own home where she could put up pictures and use the heating in the walls.

"She's very lucky," I said, and left my dad in his empty room. I only wished she had taken me with her. I wanted to know what it would be like to hang photos and nail holiday decorations to the front door.

I wanted my family.

My hands shook as I pulled on running shorts and my tennis shoes and I stretched for the first time in months. My muscles tingled and warmed and I left the house and ran. I ran fast to find her. To find her car in one of the mazes of condos, or in the parking lot of the grocery store where I met Farouk.

I ran farther than I ever had in the past, and I slowed so I wouldn't grow tired. I could have run until the sky passed from orange to deep blue. But when I didn't find her I began worrying for my dad and for me. If she wasn't there to take care of us, who would feed us and listen to us and turn her head when Dad or I did something we shouldn't have done? Who would love us despite all the bad things we did? My father would find someone else who would love him. He probably already had women who would fill Ruth's place.

But I knew those women. I knew them because they would be like the women he took me to see when I was young and he would move out for a month here, or three months there. They wore high heels with shorts and would curl my hair with hot irons and nearly burn my scalp, telling me how pretty I could be and that when I was older they would teach me how to put makeup on. I knew that if one of those women moved in, she would try to fix me like all of them had when I was a kid.

Back in my room, the heater was on. I showered and dried my hair. When I sat at my vanity table to brush my hair, I found a note.

I already miss you, Sam. I have an extra bedroom for you. Call soon, and keep me and Ernest company. All my love always, Ruth.

She'd left the phone number and drawn a little map with a star above her condo.

I folded it and put it away carefully in a drawer.

I called her in the morning as soon as I heard my dad leave. Chloe was picking me up for school.

"Wanna come over?" Ruth said.

"Of course. Yes! I miss you. You freaked me out."

"I'm so sorry to upset you, Sam. I'll pick you up from school and try to explain."

I waited through my classes, trying to focus, knowing that it would make time pass quicker. But I would still drift off, thinking about Ruth. I pictured her house a million different ways. I'd decorate my bedroom. I'd stay there as much as she'd let me. And when the final bell rang, I ran out to the school buses, where she said she'd be.

My brother was in the backseat sleeping and I held his tiny fingers while we drove. She lived in a complex near the market where Farouk and I had met. Inside, sheer white curtains were pulled back, letting in the sun, and paintings hung on the walls. It was a small apartment, but it was warm and bright and there was a photo of me on the mantel. I picked it up. It was me in my cross-country jersey, posing for team pictures.

My bedroom was bright from the afternoon light. It looked out into a small grassy yard where Ruth had planted some tiny tomato plants.

"Keep an eye on those plants. Watch for snails and those

horrible green wormy things. I'll get you binoculars so you don't have to leave the bedroom."

"What happens when I see them?"

"We'll have to have a séance and call to the antibug gods."

"Sounds good."

I looked around my room. The walls were butter yellow and the bedspread was a pale purple. It was warm and bright.

"Cozy," I said. "You're so settled. It looks like you've been here for years."

"Just a little over a month. I rented it, then moved in gradually. Pulled all my stuff from storage."

"It's amazing. We didn't have a clue."

"I had to do it."

"I know," I said, and touched the bedspread.

"You can repaint, hang posters, whatever you want in here. I just want you to feel at home."

She'd hung framed pictures on the walls. Monet's garden. *The Starry Night*.

"I like it just the way it is."

Ernest began to fuss in the other room and I started for the door.

"Sam." Ruth touched my arm. "I didn't leave you. I'll never do that. But I had to leave him. I needed a better life. A home for me and the baby. And I hoped you would come too. Of all of us, you deserve the best life." She hugged me. She nearly swallowed me in her arms. "You're a great kid. The best."

"Thank you." I breathed into her hair. "Thanks," I said as she pulled away. Ernest let out a howl. Ruth picked him up and handed him to me.

"Have some tea?" she asked as she got out the mugs. "You can walk here from your house."

"I'll run here," I said, and held my brother to me and whispered, "I promise that you're the boy I will always love the most."

"You don't have to call. I'll give you a key." She came out of the kitchen. "Is he asleep?"

"Almost." I sat still so he could sleep. "Thank you," I said again.

I went to her house as much as I could and took care of Ernest when she went out. I studied on her patio. Chloe came over too. She held my brother and promised him, "I'll be a good auntie. You can always have candy and I'll call you in sick when you want to ditch class." We painted our nails while he slept, and we cooked dinner for Ruth when she got home. We took turns lying with him on the play mat in the living room. We put him on his stomach and held our hands on his puffy diapered bottom while he used his stomach muscles to raise himself up.

"Tummy time," Ruth had called it.

"Time for tummy time. We want you to have washboard abs," said Chloe as Ernest lifted himself. "He's going to be a total stud."

"He'll be a stud because not only is he hunky, but he's nice and sweet and thoughtful." I rubbed his little doughy feet.

"We'll win a Nobel Prize if we raise a boy like that," said Chloe, picking him up and putting her face in his neck.

• • •

One afternoon, Chloe had gone and I was feeding Ernest, waiting for Ruth. There was a knock at the door and I found Dad standing there.

"No key?"

"No, kid, I'm not a VIP like you are."

He came in and watched me feed my brother. Ruth came home and greeted him cheerfully.

"Let's catch up," she said. We ordered pizza. Ruth and my dad talked about work, and Ruth and I told stories about Ernest.

"I think he's close to saying 'Sis.' "

"Is that what you're doing these afternoons while I'm gone?" Ruth said. "Deterring him from the word 'Mom'?" She pinched me.

"How about Dad?" he said.

"You can work on that," I said. He held Ernest and Ernest smiled for him. My dad smiled back.

Ruth and Dad planned doctors' appointments and talked about his weight. When it was time for bed, Dad went alone to tuck him in.

He came out and grabbed his car keys. "Kid, are you coming home tonight or should I start renting your room?"

"I think I'll just crash out here," I said. I was already in my comfy clothes, warm socks and sweatpants.

"Come home for one night. Ruth needs her apartment back."

"It's Sam's apartment too." Ruth sat on the couch with her legs tucked under her. Her arms were folded, but she smiled.

"Sam, come home," he said sharply.

"Okay," I said, and gathered my books and shoes. I kissed Ruth and crept into the baby's room. He was cooing at the mobile of cats and mice and slices of cheese Ruth and I had hung.

"Night." I kissed his cheek and I tickled his belly. "Go to sleep before Mom catches you."

My house was cold and silent as we walked in. Maybe, like that girl had told me in elementary school, you could trap souls in a place, but soon they found their way out.

"Tired, kid?"

"A bit."

"Do you miss me?" He stood in the kitchen with the fluorescent lights above his head hissing and making his skin gray.

"I miss all of us together. I miss having a family."

"I'm here," he said, and hugged me. "I miss you, too." He kissed the top of my head. He smelled spicy sweet like he always had. "Now, I'm beat. I'll give you a lift to school tomorrow."

He walked up the stairs and left me alone in the bright gray kitchen. I turned the light off and listened in the silence for the voices of people I had loved within these walls. I listened hard, and heard my father moving in his room, getting ready for bed. The others were free.

And so I didn't miss Farouk as much as I had. It had been easy to let him go because I told myself those words he'd said in Farsi were terrible words. I told myself he'd said that I was hopeless, or unlovable, or ugly. And when I missed him I would listen to those words again and feel all the hurt I was sure he meant. And that was how I got over freezing in the hall when I saw him coming. It was how I managed not to leave math class in the middle when he would turn and talk to a girl sitting next to him.

And I was okay at the end of the year as the mornings grew hotter and I began wearing shorts and T-shirts and pulling my hair up into a heavy ponytail. I was fine, fine, looking forward to the summer.

"What should we do this summer? Should we go to the south of France and then Italy or the Bahamas?" Chloe said.

"What about Oakland? Road trip, and we have a place to stay."

"That's what I like to hear. We'll hang out on Telegraph and take important political stands."

"And we'll train. We'll run, wherever we are."

"I'm not much of a runner," she said.

"You'll be training with the best."

A week before school ended, I went to see the coach. I knew she'd be in her office, though the locker room was empty and the season was over.

"I'm going for varsity next year," I said as I stood in her doorway like I had when I complained of my stomach or a headache.

She looked at me and smiled. "You need to work hard, Sam. Your times need to be consistent. The girls are tough."

"I will."

"Okay," she said, and stood. She put her hand on my shoulder and looked at me. "You have to believe. I believe in you. You're a beautiful runner, with a long stride and an easy rhythm. But I can see that when you run, you don't think this. And then you run like you see yourself—just not that great. That isn't you. You're fast. You're a true runner. Do you believe that?"

"I do."

"I do too," she said, and released me for the summer.

And I was okay. I was okay until the day before school let out and I began my walk home and saw Farouk leaning against his car, and I thought: He's waiting for me. Finally, my waiting had paid off and I wouldn't have to be just okay anymore, and so I walked to him without looking around me for cars or for people or that Persian girl, who reached him first.

I was close enough to smell her, vanilla and musk, and I was close enough to see her kiss him and tell him those words I'd heard in my own head.

"Asheghetam lakpost," she said.

And I was ready for him to walk away from her, and I felt so lucky to be so close to him. To catch him as he understood those words.

But he kissed her once on the mouth, and then again on each eye, and into her ear he returned the words, but in English this time.

"I love you, turtle," he said, and kissed her again.

about the author

melissa lion earned an M.F.A. in creative writing from Saint Mary's College of California, where she received the Agnes Butler Scholarship for Literary Excellence. Her stories have appeared in the *Santa Monica Review, Other Voices* and *The Crucifix Is Down,* an anthology published by Red Hen Press. Melissa Lion is a native Californian who burns easily in the sun.